The DREAMATICS

Michelle Cuevas

 ROCKY POND BOOKS

ROCKY POND BOOKS
An imprint of Penguin Random House LLC, New York

Ⓟ

First published in the United States of America by Rocky Pond Books,
an imprint of Penguin Random House LLC, 2023
Copyright © 2023 by Michelle Cuevas

Visit us online at PenguinRandomHouse.com.

Library of Congress Cataloging-in-Publication Data is available.

Printed in the United States of America

ISBN 9780593532225

1st Printing

LSCH

Design by Jason Henry
Text set in Celeste Pro

For Indy, my dream dog

CHAPTERS

Cast List

(Dreamatis Personae)

Luna, a dreamer

Matías and Ted, her parents

Murph, a beloved dog

Dormir, a lowly theatre assistant

The Director

Circadia, lighting department

Nox, set designer

Tuck, costumes

Dozer, a handyman

Reverie, an actress

The Forty Winks Orchestra

Winks, conductor

The Unseen Playwright

The Bad Dreams

Coco, the worst

Greeph, a poet

The Counting Sheep

The Memory Vault Keepers

The Questling Beast

PROLOGUE

*O*nstage, a dream is unfolding.

The theatre's lighting department has outdone itself—somehow managing to perfectly re-create the amber glow of a late-afternoon sun, right down to the dappled and dancing light through the leaves. The set builders have grown giant sunflowers that tower on the stage, and the actors have transformed themselves into dragon-sized bumblebees, emerging from the flowers with their fuzzy bodies covered in golden pollen. Even the air in the theatre feels crisp and edged with the smell of apples.

A great wind starts blowing, and yellow leaves begin swirling around the stage, some blowing out into the theatre and over the velvet-covered seats. The leaves change to snow, and the stage is transformed—now a lone lantern glows through the fluffy flakes, the ground sparkles like a million tiny moons, and the air smells of nutmeg, gingerbread, and a hint of pine.

This is the magic of the theatre; the way the creaking floorboards seem to speak in their own language; the way every prop, light, and velvet seat seem to know the audi-

1

ence by name; the way a stage can also be bumblebees and lanterns, cinnamon, and snow.

This is where dreams are written, *says the creaking floor.*

This is where dreams are born, built, brought to life, *say the blinking lights.*

This . . . is the Lunarian Grand.

But then, the sweet smells begin to sour, and the big, beautiful flakes of snow begin to whip in the wind, turning to hail, then lashing sleet. The theatre goes cold—colder than cold—causing icicles to form below the box seats and balcony.

Crunch.

Crunch.

Crunch.

Something is stalking through the snow. Something is crushing fallen branches. Something is howling with a cry like screeching tires. The footsteps come closer and closer, carrying something wrong, something bad, something that smells of fear and darkness and something worse, far worse, too awful to even imagine.

"Cut!" yells the Director. "Wake up!"

"Wake up. Wake up!" join in the rest of the cast and crew.

"Wake up," I whisper, less sure than the rest. "Wake up, it's only a dream . . ."

A BRIEF EXPLANATION
OF THE PROLOGUE

*O*nly a dream? you're probably saying. *Was that whole prologue just a dream? But I HATE when writers do that. It's lazy! Just stay in reality, pal.*

Don't worry, I totally agree. Lazy, lazy, lazy.

Well . . . that is . . . except in this one, specific, very particular case. Because, you see, dreams *are* our reality.

Hey! Come back. Where are you going? Okay, okay, I can see I'm starting to lose you. How to explain, how to explain . . .

Let's see . . . have you ever woken up from a dream and thought, *What was THAT? My auntie Gertrude shaped like a giant platypus waddling through my middle school while singing the word "farfanoogle" over and over?* Well, that dream? That was us! Or a dream theatre just like us. We built the middle school set, one of our actors played Aunt Gertrude the platypus, and our orchestra performed the Farfanoogle Waltz in Zzz Minor.

That's because we are the members of the Lunarian Grand Theatre, affectionately referred to among ourselves as the Dreamatics. Every night we perform the dreams of one Luna Grande, age ten and three-quarters. Well, every night until tragedy struck and changed everything forever.

But I'm getting ahead of myself. Let's start at the beginning . . .

Chapter One

THE WEATHER CLOSET

Someone hadn't fully closed a jar of winter in the weather closet, and everything was covered in drifts of snow. *Again.*

Frost glazed the bottles of wind and the jugs of raining rain, and I had to dig to find the glass orbs of sunsets I'd been sent for in the first place. I finally found the one that Nox had told me to find—"colored peach pie with clouds à la mode, fading into a melted sherbet horizon."

"Team, your desire for a snowball fight later," said the Director, "is not an excuse to leave winter open in the set department again and give . . . uh . . . Whozamacallit here frostbite."

I smiled and shook the snowflakes from my overalls. Sure, call me Whozamacallit. Or Whatsername. Or So-and-So. I answered to them all. Who needs to learn the name of the lowliest of low assistants?

(It's Dormir, by the way. My name, that is.)

"Sorry, boss," said Nox, our set designer. "My bad. Also, you said you wanted to change the snow for tonight's performance? What kind of snow d'ya want?"

"Ugh, must I do everything?" asked the Director. "Just make it romantic. Make it fun." She was wearing one of her usual stress-related T-shirts, which always featured things like a picture of a lightbulb saying "I'm burnt out!" or a head of lettuce saying "Romaine calm!" Today was another classic—a cat shouting "DON'T STRESS MEOWT!"

"We've got all the kinds of snowy precipitation," continued Nox. "Ice pellets, blizzard, squall, thundersnow . . ."

"Do *you* think 'thundersnow' sounds romantic?" asked the Director.

"I wouldn't know," said Nox, putting her dirty work gloves on her hips.

"Something unique," continued the Director. "Something poetic."

"Unique . . . poetic . . . well, we have one thing, fairly rare," said Nox. "It's called watermelon snow."

"And that is . . . ?"

"It's technically caused by a red-colored green algae called *Chlamydomonas nivalis,*" said Nox with the poetry of a snowplow.

The Director stared, bewildered.

"It's pink," said Nox. "Pink snow. It happens in the real world."

I didn't hear the end of the conversation, as I had plenty

of my own work to do before the theatre opened for the night.

Not that I was complaining. I may have been a lowly-low assistant, but I was lowly-low at the *Lunarian Grand*, which was, in my humble opinion, the most majestic, magical, beautiful theatre in the entire universe. I was sawing, nailing, painting, and rigging most of the time, sure, but I was also part of the *show*. I felt the tingling excitement every time the houselights dimmed, knew every line by heart, and whispered them under my breath from the wings, loving every moment, but knowing that I would never be in the spotlight.

You will never bask in that kind of glow, I'd tell myself.

You will never capture moments, say things unsaid, stir hearts, feel the thrill of the unknown.

You will always be only what you are: a lowly stage-hand, a set painter, an assistant to all, but never the star.

Still, I thought. *Still.*

Even a dream like me was allowed to dream.

Chapter Two
THE LUNARIAN GRAND

"If it isn't the wizardess of illumination," I said to my best friend, Circadia, opening the door to the lighting department. "Need anything before the show?"

Circadia, her giant eyes magnified even more by thick glasses, looked up from her table of various-shaped lightbulbs. She had a giant-insect-genius-who-may-accidentally-demolish-the-theatre vibe about her.

"Dormir!" she said. "Check it out."

"Uh, which one?" I asked, my eyes traveling around the room.

Every shelf, every wall, and most of the ceiling were covered with lamps, sconces, chandeliers, and lanterns. There was an acorn lamp that made the entire theatre fill with giant shadows of trees, a bat light that made stalactites appear on the ceiling and balcony, and an orb pendant filled with fog that could engulf the space in mist. They ranged from pea-sized to a chandelier the size of a blue whale.

"I think I've got it," said Circadia, pointing to the whale. "It illuminates the stage with the exact light of being underwater, with a hint of sky far, far above. Took me ages to get it just right."

Circadia turned on the whale lamp, and even though I was used to her brilliance, the glow that filled the room still caught my breath—it was like we'd been plunged into deep blue-green water, and near the ceiling—which now looked like sunshine and water-blurred clouds—there were darting schools of fish like specks of twinkling silver. A jellyfish floated by, but when I reached out to touch it, my hand went right through it. Just another trick of the light.

"One of my new almost-favorites," I said. I licked my lips and could swear I tasted salt water.

"Noted," said Circadia.

This, I knew, was Circadia's way of knowing someone better—much like anyone else might ask about a favorite band or movie or book, Circadia wanted to know about favorite kinds of light. Circadia's favorite, which changed constantly, was currently "the flame of an over-toasted marshmallow."

After my visit with Circadia, I checked in with Tuck (favorite light: the way sequins glittered onstage) in the costume department. Tuck was to wardrobe what Circadia was to light, and he made costumes that could transform any actor's details—change their voice, walk, mannerisms, even their smell. The walls were lined with spools in every color, the strings all made from threads of memory.

"Need anything before the show?" I asked.

"Ooh, yes, could you try on this dragon scale cape?" said Tuck. "I'm having some trouble with the pyrotechnics."

I let Tuck fit the hooded cape made of green scales over my head, and as soon as he did, I felt a tickling in my throat. I coughed once, twice, then POOF! A giant flame shot out of my mouth.

"Perfect," said Tuck, removing the costume. "You okay?"

"It feels like I burned my tongue on hot soup."

"Intriguing," Tuck said, making a note. "What flavor soup?"

Next on my preshow rounds was Nox in sets (favorite light: moonbeams on dewy grass). Both her hands were filled with watering cans and she was holding one in her mouth as well, so I grabbed a can and started helping her with the watering.

"These buildings are coming in real nice," I said, looking at the saplings, which were shaped like wee skyscrapers.

The sets in the set department were planted by Nox as little seeds, then watered, fed, and grown to full beauty and size. It took just as long as building by hand but made everything seem more natural and realistic.

"Let's sing," said Nox. "They prefer jazz, really helps them grow."

And so, we sang:

"With soft rain showers and sunlight
Your walls grow strong, your angles right
Now floor by floor and room by room
Become a building in full bloom"

After helping Nox I walked toward the lobby, where I ran into Dozer (favorite light: a night-light). Dozer was our handyman, and in charge of changing the nightly show titles on the marquee. His name was fitting since he was almost always napping; most days he even fell asleep as he was putting the giant letters into place on the marquee. Luckily, the Lunarian Grand would usually just get exasperated and change its marquee itself.

Entering the lobby, I stared at the letters on the marquee. "We're putting on a show called *POO DAY AT SCHOOL*?" I asked. But then I realized what had happened.

"Dozer!" I shouted up to him on his ladder. His head was resting on the top rung. "Hey Dozer, you fell asleep again. I think you've left the H and the T out of the word *PHOTO*."

"I'm on it," said Dozer, not opening his eyes.

Next, I did a final check backstage before heading to the main theatre. Lanterns lined the hallways backstage, halls that I'd always thought might be endless. There were rooms filled with all kinds of familiar voices and laughter, rooms with school assignments wallpapering the walls, and rooms that held secrets that echoed like whispers down a well. One room housed a giant clock, and instead of numbers, it had degrees of sleepiness of Luna, each sounding like a distant relation of Sleepy from Snow White.

Drowsy.

Alert.

Perky.

Tuckered.

Overtired.

Sluggish.

Invigorated.

One Eye Open.

Sprightly.

Fatigued.

Energetic.

Asleep.

Were I Snow White, Asleep would be my favorite. Asleep was where the action was. Asleep was where the Dreamatics really shined.

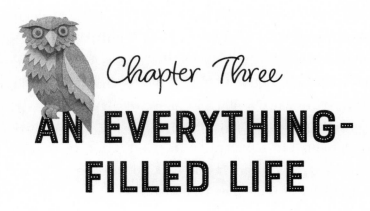

Chapter Three

AN EVERYTHING-FILLED LIFE

The truth was, the Dreamatics shined because of Luna. How could we not? Our shows were based on the Everything-Filled Life of a girl named after the moon.

And what, exactly, is an Everything-Filled Life?

Well, in Luna's case, it was her teachers, her friends, and her neighbors. It was her favorite songs, and books, and beaches. But most of all, it was her family: her father Ted, her father Matías, and her beloved dog, Murph.

Of course, an Everything-Filled Life wouldn't be complete without vast and varied interests, and Luna was no slouch in that department. In fact, she had a new most-favorite interest just about every other week and threw herself into them with wild abandon. There was her bee-keeping phase, her acronym-collecting phase, her map-making phase, and her magician phase. She even had a tree phase, and let me tell you, those are some fascinating plants. She would read facts to Murph from books, things like "Trees carry time in their rings," and "In those rings you can read about ancient weather." She said that trees are connected and can even communicate. Trees take care of one another—one tree will nourish another when injured by feeding it nutrients through their roots, keeping it alive, bringing it back to full bloom. Who knew trees had such a social life?

But Luna's most recent passion was the one that interested me the most, for obvious reasons.

"Dad, how do dreams work?" Luna asked while eating her cereal and, clearly, thinking some deep thoughts.

"Hmmm," said her father Ted, sipping his coffee. "I suppose that technically speaking, it all takes place inside the temporal lobe of the brain, where the hippocampus has a central role in our ability to remember, imagine, and dream. Experts theorize that dreaming is a way to store important memories."

"Well, why do I keep dreaming about the Bermuda Triangle then?" said Luna, rolling her eyes. Her father Ted, a math teacher, tended to think about things in the most literal terms.

"What do you think, Papa?" Luna asked, turning to her father Matías.

"Ah, the eternal question," said Matías, staring off into the distance. "The most important part of a dream is the mystery, the one beyond reach or reason or language. A dream," he continued, "takes a while to rise in the morning, especially when it has not had its breakfast."

Luna looked from one dad to the other, realizing that perhaps she needed a more neutral source for this information. She got down under the table and lay flat on the floor on her stomach until she was nose to nose with Murph. The dog wagged his tail with joy.

"So, what do you dream about?" asked Luna.

Murph, in reply, licked Luna's nose.

Luna placed her hands on each side of Murph's face. "Just tell me. I won't tell anyone, I promise.

"Okay, fine," said Luna when Murph continued his silently loving stare. "I'll just guess what you dream, and you can blink when I'm right. Ready? Okay. Let's see . . . do you dream about . . . Stan?"

Stan was Murph's favorite squeak toy, shaped like a carrot.

"No blink for Stan," said Luna. "Do you dream about . . . squirrels?"

No blink for squirrels.

"Do you dream about the dishwasher?"

Murph was deathly afraid of the dishwasher. But no blink.

"Do you dream about the smells at the beach?"
No blink.

"Do you dream about watermelon?"
Murph loved watermelon. But no blink.

"Do you dream about running through the sprinkler

on a summer day? Delivery people and the treats they leave for you with the packages? Your favorite flavors of cheese??"

No blink.

No blink.

No blink.

But Murph *did* dream, Luna was sure of it. That was because he slept in her bed, and when he dreamed, he twitched his eyes and snout, made little happy whines, and moved his paws like he was swimming or running or digging a hole.

Luna and Murph were best friends—they shared the same pillow, head-to-head, and often woke up from sleep to check that the other was still there. Murph was like Luna's second shadow as she moved around the house, step for step, room to room. He kept watch at the window for her when she was away and did a butt-wiggling, tail-wagging dance of joy when she returned. Sometimes, when she was doing homework or watching a movie, he'd go to his pile of toys and bring her one, laying it on her lap. He couldn't exactly speak, but Luna was pretty sure he was saying, *I am not a rich dog. I don't have much. This is one of my only possessions, but I'd like you to have it, just the same.*

And because they were best friends, Luna really did want to know what Murph dreamed about, so when her family made their weekly library trip, Luna checked out every book she could find about dreams. She read about dreams made of sunlight and plums, and dreams made of ice; dreams that glowed in the dark, dreams made of unwound fingerprints, dreams that flew away like a lost kite string. She read that some dreams followed you all day, purring against your windows, lounging on your roof, lingering after dawn. Dreams like dew hanging on a spider's web. Dreams like a music box's last notes. Dreams like an old firefly, blinking its last light.

But the part that intrigued her the most was in a section about non-human dreaming, and the most recent research about dogs. It read:

Latest research shows that when dogs sleep, they are dreaming about their humans. Since dogs are generally extremely attached to their human owners, it's likely your dog is dreaming of your face, your smell, and of pleasing or annoying you.

And so that night as Murph dreamed, Luna watched; she watched his eyes and whiskers flutter, his chest rise and fall, his mouth let out the tiniest whimper. It was probably impossible, Luna thought, not to love someone—human or dog or anyone else—once you'd seen their eyes tremble in an unknown dream. And when Murph started moving his paws, paddling through the invisible air of sleep, Luna thought of the words she had read: *Research shows that when dogs sleep, they are dreaming about their humans.*

All this time she'd seen Murph dreaming, she had thought he was imagining toys and treats. But no. The truth was far better, far sweeter, had far deeper roots. Murph wasn't escaping from something. He wasn't racing after a ball in a game of fetch. He wasn't chasing rabbits through the long grass.

He dreams of running, she thought, her heart in full bloom, *toward me.*

Chapter Four

FORTY WINKS

It was almost bedtime for Luna, which meant it was almost showtime for us back at the Lunarian Grand. After my rounds checking in with each department, I arrived inside the theatre itself, which never failed to amaze me. The Lunarian Grand was made of dark wood, with seats of soft leather and curtains of rich velvet. It smelled of sawdust, and cotton candy, and was lit by warm globe lights around the stage (my personal favorite light), giving a feeling of perpetual twilight. But this set-up wasn't always the case, as the Lunarian Grand tended to have, shall we say . . . a mind of its own. It would redecorate at whim, adding new box seats shaped like boats, or train cars, or fluffy clouds, and frequently changed the two statues that flanked the top corners of the stage— I'd seen them as octopuses, giant books, trees of owls, gryphons, and currently, two foxes holding umbrellas. The Lunarian also grew new rooms and re-wallpapered the old ones whenever it was bored. Even the hallways sometimes changed—we called them cunning corridors and perfidious passageways—since you'd enter one, knowing your destination, and end up somewhere completely different than last time.

But mostly, Lunarian pranks aside, stepping into the theatre always gave me a feeling of wonder, mystery, and most of all, magic. I only had a few minutes to take in this glowing splendor before I heard shouts coming from the orchestra pit.

"Dormir!" shouted the voice. "Dormir, I'm down here! In the orchestra pit. The PIT OF DESPAIR."

The voice could only belong to our beloved Winks, orchestra conductor of the Forty Winks Orchestra, who put the "dramatic" in Dreamatics and had a heavy Phantom-of-the-Opera vibe. (Lotta capes.) (Favorite light: a lit candelabra, the kind that made everyone look both softer around the edges and also more sinister.)

"Dormir, darling," he continued, "we need more music stands for the percussive section. No hurry, though the cymbalists *are* improvising with nothing to hold their music. The horror. The HORROR!"

I looked into the pit and saw that the cymbal players had sheet music taped to the inside of their cymbals, attempting to read it between crashes. Yikes. I ran backstage and grabbed the extra stands, then ran back to the pit. I had to wait in the shadows until they finished the piece they were rehearsing, and by the end, my cheeks and chin were wet with tears.

"Wonderful," said Winks, looking over at me. "Feel those EMOTIONS!"

"Not like I could avoid it even if I tried," I said, wiping away the tears. I understood how it all worked, but I'd never truly gotten used to the way the orchestra manipulated emotions—useful for Luna's dreams, of course, but it still always took me by surprise. "It's just . . . that song," I said. "It made me feel like . . . like I just cooked a huge dinner, and dropped it on the floor, and then everyone I know got together and cooked a new dinner . . . and I was so sad, and then happy, and then just crying from a weird mix of the two."

"Hmmm," said Winks. "Close. We were going for: Someone told me my crush doesn't like me, but later they pass me a note in class to say, 'Um, yes I do, kind of maybe.' Perhaps we need to tweak the violins . . ."

The manipulation of emotions wasn't the only surprising thing about the Forty Winks Orchestra—all forty of them also looked just like Winks, the conductor. The only difference was that all the musicians were basically playing themselves as instruments—the horn section had giant horn-shaped noses, the strings had antlers strung with strings, and the harpist was strumming her own elaborately long cat-like whiskers.

"Such talent!" Winks would always say about them. "And SO VERY ATTRACTIVE."

I'd always been impressed by the orchestra members' ability to transform into their instruments. In truth, we were all magical creatures at the Lunarian Grand, and all *technically* had the ability to change into any form, to morph like clay. But most of our jobs didn't require anything of the sort. And not everyone had a talent or knack for this particular skill. Winks, for example, would always lay a dramatic hand across his forehead and proclaim, "I just have too much individual style to alter my form!"

But even the orchestra members, moldable as they were, couldn't hold a candle to the ones who shifted shape into new characters every night on the dream stage.

I'm referring, of course, to my favorites:

The actors.

The thespians.

The *stars.*

Chapter Five

SUGAR-SPUN SNOW

The actors were—in my personal opinion—the greatest, most wonderful, most integral part of the theatre.

"I just love the way they change shape," I said to Circadia . . . or Dozer . . . or pretty much anyone who would listen at all hours of the day. "I mean, there are good actors, but then there are those who are truly great."

"What's the difference?" yawned Dozer. I'd told them my theories a bazillion times, but Dozer had usually nodded off by the time I'd made my point.

"Well," I'd tell him again, "you know when someone's asleep, and they can't really tell who someone is in their dream? They wake up and say, *I had the craziest dream about someone who was a mix of my grandmother and my kindergarten teacher and maybe . . . a horse?* Well, the actor playing that character just isn't a very good actor. But with a *great* actor, the dreamer knows, for sure, who they're seeing. The way the actor morphs, and changes shape, and adopts the exact voice and mannerisms and smell and . . . well, the dreamer just *knows*. Without a doubt. And that's pure, perfect, dream-theatre magic."

Which was why I felt triple-excited-with-a-cherry-on-top when after all my preshow rounds, I learned I'd get to interact with the actors at our nightly performance. And by interact, I mean stand at the side of the stage and whisper lines to the actors if they forgot them. It's called being "on book." And my favorite actor to be "on book" for was Reverie (favorite light: a spotlight). She was the most talented, most transformable, and most absorbed in her craft. Really, it's understandable how she never seemed to have time to learn her lines. Which meant—yay!—I got to help.

And that night, the show was going to be a Reverie-starring spec-tac-u-lar. She was reprising her role as "Luna's New Crush at School," and let me tell you, the way she slouched during the scenes in math class? WOWZERS. If she didn't win a Snory Award for Worst Posture, it would be the bummer of the century.

"Okay," said the Director, "a few points of business before tonight's performance. Our audience has discovered the snooze button, which means we'll be doing at least three encores. Also, tomorrow is Saturday, so be prepared for a matinee nap. Let's gather round."

We all gathered in a circle, linking our arms and shouting the theatre's motto toward the rafters.

"Teamwork Makes the Dream Work!"

"Hey, uh . . . hit the hay," I said quietly to Reverie as she sashayed past me. I'd heard that in theatres in Luna's world they said "break a leg" before performances, but we all agreed it seemed kind of morbid.

Nox's scenery for the performance was an award-worthy effort as well—a winter semiformal school dance, but not quite. The interior of the humdrum school gym had somehow mixed seamlessly with a scene from Narnia (Luna's current favorite book), and a lone lantern glowed as the snow fell in fat flakes. The air was scented with a hint of pine and wood fire as Circadia's lighting scheme came alive with infinite snow sparkling under a moon-shaped chandelier.

I held my script and took my place in the prompt corner behind the curtain. It was a deep purple-blue velvet, and before the show it remained closed, covered in ornate beads in the shape of open eyes.

"Aaaaaand *action,*" said the Director.

As the curtains parted, the beaded eyes changed from open to closed. This meant Luna was officially asleep. It was a small detail, but it thrilled me every time.

And then, the orchestra music swelled.

And then, the spotlight slowly came up.

And then, all the world was *Reverie.*

Onstage, Reverie-as-Crush walked forward, the only sound the crunching of snow under her feet. She had changed both shape and size, and now stood heads above me, sandy-brown hair falling over one eye, wearing a soccer uniform in neon green.

"I heard you wanted to dance with me, here at the Snowball Let's-Waltz-in-Winter Dance," said Reverie-as-Crush. Her voice was much lower and goofier than usual. "And that you want us to have our first kiss as the fake snow slowly falls around us and the smell of toasted marshmallows inexplicably fills the air. And my answer," said Reverie-as-Crush, "is . . . um. My answer is . . .

"Line," she whispered in my direction, like a ventriloquist, hardly moving her lips.

"No," I whispered from my position at the edge of the stage.

"*Line,*" yell-whispered Reverie, more emphatically.

"*No,*" I yell-whispered back.

"Line *please,*" snarled Reverie.

"No!"

"LINE! LINE! I NEED MY LINE!"

"YOUR LINE IS 'NO'!" I yelled. The entire cast and crew turned to stare at me as I attempted to disappear behind the curtain.

"CUT!" yelled the Director. "Classic dream, very confusing. Next act, folks."

I knew that in the lobby, the theatre would be quickly changing the marquee—from SNOWBALL OF REJECTION to THE DOG ATE MY DIARY while Dozer supervised/napped nearby.

Behind the curtain, I helped change the set, which was

26

now a backyard washed in early morning light. When the Director yelled action, Reverie—now in the shape of Luna's dog, Murph—ran onstage with a book in her teeth. She started ripping out pages, which were filled with curlicue hearts and problems and secrets.

"Ooh," I said, speaking to Circadia, who was now at my side adjusting various lights. "This is deep."

"What is?" asked Circadia.

"Well," I explained, "that's Luna's diary, and Murph is now burying it. Like . . . burying feelings. It's a metaphor. Or something."

"Incredible," said Circadia. "You truly understand these shows. You shouldn't be a lowly assistant, Dormir, you should be writing these things."

"That's silly," I said, bending over to pick up a pebble that flew off stage as Reverie-as-Murph was digging a hole. "I could never . . ."

Though truth be told, I wondered if I could. I knew more than anyone about the Everything-Filled Life these shows were based on; why, sometimes, I thought maybe I knew Luna Grande, age ten and three-quarters, better than I knew myself.

Chapter Six
THE DREAM COLLECTOR

The Director yelled "That's a wrap! She's awake!" after Luna's dream, and I crept away into the darkness behind the stage. I'd always found it comforting—the way I was able to navigate the darkened backstage, even when it was littered with props and sets. I suspected it was how it felt to navigate around furniture in the dark in a home you'd lived in forever. Not that I'd ever had a home, exactly. But I could imagine.

I made my way beyond the backstage and down the hallways, running my hand along the walls covered in endless, framed playbills of the various dreams over the years. Like all photos or artwork in the Lunarian, the scenes depicted remained the same, but the time of day and weather changed to fit whatever was happening in Luna's current world. Some playbills were faded, depending on how difficult the dream was to remember, but others remained bright, washed in sunlight or moonlight or the glint of fresh rain. There was . . .

THE ONE WITH THE GIANT BUG CAROUSEL

THE ONE IN THE EVERTHING-IS-EDIBLE FOREST

THE ONE WITH THE (YIKES!) BERUMUDA TRIANGLE

THE ONE WITH ENDLESS PACKING FOR A TRIP THAT NEVER COMES

THE ONE WHERE LUNA IS FLYING A FEW FEET ABOVE THE GROUND

THE ONE WHERE LUNA FORGOT THE BIG TEST (AND VARIOUS SEQUELS)

THE ONE WITH THE PET OCTOPUS

THE ONE WITHOUT A MOON

THE ONE WITH TOO MANY MOONS

Finally, I came to my place, my secret space, the closest thing I had to a home.

"It's not much, but at least it's . . . covered in spider-webs," I said to nobody at all.

The set storage room—if you could call it a room—was a mix between a wonderland and a dream graveyard. The room was high-ceilinged and endless (at least I'd never found the end) and filled with hills and valleys of wild scenery—candy forests with gumdrop mushrooms, ice gardens with frozen sculptures, circus tents set up for tarot readings, and a carriage in the shape of a crescent moon once pulled by actors transformed into flying rabbits. Just beyond a carousel made of insects, was my favorite place of all: the beach. It wasn't a beach exactly, but it did have a long stretch of sand, blue plastic waves, and the smell of salt, seaweed, and suntan lotion. The breezes blew here, and Circadia had let me borrow a chandelier that made ever-changing, fluffy clouds float up near the ceiling. Sometimes they were shaped like elephants or whales, sailboats or steam trains; sometimes I saw the shape of a girl, a dog, and a lowlier-than-low theatre assistant. The dog cloud would blow around the other two, licking their faces and fetching cloud sticks.

But then the clouds would blow on a breeze, and change shape, and I would once again be alone. Alone in my little castle made of sand, a fort of my own, just big enough for me and my growing collection. There was probably a rule against it in some obscure dream handbook, but I tried to collect one souvenir from every performance. The shelves that lined the inside of my fort were crowded with buttons, marbles, wishing pennies, scraps of paper, half-used crayons, and beautiful, never-dying flowers.

This place was my secret. It's where I wrote my own little shows, each one the same—starring me, having imaginary conversations with Luna. I'd tell her about my day, and she'd tell me about hers. We'd make up games, romp with Murph, and sing songs. Luna and I shared a love of duets, and in my opinion the theatre didn't perform enough musical dreams.

I placed the rock from tonight's performance, the one kicked up by Reverie-as-Murph-the-dog, onto the shelf in a position of honor, right beside my favorite item of all, the one I called the First Walk Seashell. It looked like an average shell, nothing special really, sea-worn and greenish gray. What made it special was *when* it was from—the first walk Luna ever took with her new puppy Murph, on a beach many years ago.

See, Luna was a collector just like me, and in her world, every time she went on a walk with Murph, she picked up a souvenir—a pebble, a shell, a piece of glass worn dull by the sea. She'd hold it out to Murph and say, "What do you think?" And Murph would sniff and lick every inch in approval. Of course, not everything that happened in Luna's life ended up written into a dream, but that first walk with Murph did. It was so special to her, Luna dreamed it over and over. And after one of those dreams, I sneaked to the prop table and slipped the First Walk Seashell into my pocket. It felt different than the other items I'd collected—maybe because it wasn't just a wild dream creation but a real memory from the real world. It had been in Luna's hand, then in her dream, and now it was mine.

I know what you're thinking: Dormir, you're *clearly* in love with Luna. Or perhaps you're in love with . . . her dog?

But that's not exactly the case.

I'm not in love with her. Or Murph, for that matter.

I'm in love with . . . well, I suppose I'm in love with her Everything-Filled Life.

Chapter Seven

FRIDAY-FLAVORED POPCORN

And all the Everything I loved about Luna's Everything-Filled Life was brought to us, in vivid detail, each day via the Daily Newsreel.

The Daily Newsreel took place in the screening room, which was cozy and warm, with plush seats and furry blankets. There was even a popcorn machine that changed flavors depending on the mood—my favorite was Friday-Flavored; it tasted like the expectation of sleeping in, and chocolate-chip pancakes, and an entire weekend's worth of fun. Every day all the Dreamatics gathered together in this mini movie theatre to watch a highlight reel of Luna's entire day—her ups and her downs, her triumphs and her heartaches. We watched her learn to ride a bike, and learn to patch a skinned knee from falling off a bike. We watched her make friends, lose friends, and everything in between.

It was in that very screening room that I first heard the Nighty-Night Song. I remember it well—it was around Christmas, and the screening room had self-decorated in shades of deep green and red, with holly and berries around the screen and the sound of a crackling fire filling the air. There was even a jolly tree trimmed in ornaments of Luna's current favorite things—crunchy leaves, paper cranes, kiwi fruits, and bats. The popcorn machine was churning out special popcorn that tasted like cinnamon, sledding, and the pitter-patter of reindeer hooves on a roof.

On the screen that day, we all watched as Luna celebrated the end of preschool, getting picked up, and rushing home to greet her toys. But to her shock, there was a special surprise waiting for her: a little ball of scruffy-haired, rescue-dog love. She called the puppy Murph, and over the months and years to come, every time I saw them together, I got the same syrupy-sweet green-eyed feeling in the pit of my stomach—something at the intersection of wonder, and love, and a wish for it to all be mine.

I watched Murph grow from a puppy, with his too-large paws, super-soft ears, and desire to chew every sock in sight, into a constant and steadfast companion. He waited each day for Luna to come home, and when she did, they would read books, play fetch, laugh, and snuggle.

And me?

Well, I was hooked.

What must it be like, I marveled, *to lie in a patch of warm grass, giggling uncontrollably while a dog licks your face? To share an ice-cream cone? To have someone wait and watch and spin in circles when you came home? To be tucked in together, each kissed on the forehead goodnight? What must it feel like to be loved like that,* I wondered. *To bask in that kind of glow?*

Every night since that first night, Luna sang Murph the Nighty-Night Song. Each night the chorus was the same, but Luna would change the words to the rest of the song to match whatever she and Murph did that day. I still remember the words to her very first Nighty-Night Song. I remember because they were perfect.

Goodnight
I love you
I'll see you in the morning

When it's light
And bright
And you've finished all your snoring

Sweet dreams of dog parks
And eating flowers on our walks
Sweet dreams of chewing socks
Chasing pigeons, scaring flocks

Sweet dreams of good-boy treats
And sniffing every butt you meet
Sweet dreams of belly rubs
Of mud puddles and bath-time tubs

Sweet dreams of sunny naps
Of flying wings and treasure maps
Sweet dreams of me and you
Sweet dreams the whole night through

Goodnight
I love you
I'll see you in the morning

When it's light
And bright
And you've finished all your snoring

Chapter Eight
THE SNORYS

"I think it's a ghost," said Circadia.

"My current theory," said Dozer, "is that there *is* no playwright, and little birds and mice write the plays, like in a fairy tale."

"Intriguing," I said, laughing. "Mine is that the Unseen part doesn't so much mean unseen as unsee-able. As in . . . dum, dum, DUM: *invisible.*

We were lounging in the screening room, talking about one of our favorite topics: the Unseen Playwright. Mysterious and slightly ominous name, right? As the name would suggest, nobody had ever seen the Unseen Playwright, but each day, like clockwork, after the News-reel aired in the screening room, there would be a flurry of weather—wind or hail or rain—called a Brain Storm. After that, a script would come shooting through an air pipe system known as the Pipe Dream, and land smack in the Director's hands. Copies would be dispersed, costumes woven, sets grown and harvested, and a new dream would make its debut.

"I think it's fireflies blinking out the scripts in Morse code," said Circadia.

"I think it's a magical, self-writing quill pen," yawned Dozer.

"I think it's a room full of cats typing on typewriters," I said.

It was the same question we'd been asking for years, and we had an evolving list of theories including such possibilities as the Unseen Playwright being the returned spirit of Shakespeare, and the Unseen Playwright actually being Dozer—that his habit of constantly falling asleep was a cover and he was secretly writing dreams with his eyes closed. But the truth was, we had no idea who, or what, wrote the Dreamatics' plays.

"Maybe this will be the year the Unseen Playwright shows up and accepts their writing award," said Circadia.

"Maybe they *have* shown up," I said, winking. "But, ya know . . . *invisible.*"

"Look, I could discuss this forever," said Circadia, "but we'd better get a move on and go see Tuck in costumes. I don't want all the good ensembles to be taken."

Everyone, including us, wanted to look their best— and with good reason.

It was the most wonderful, funniest, greatest day of the year.

It was the day of . . . the Snory Awards.

✳   ✳   ✳

"Take your seats, take your seats," said the Director. "And welcome to the Tenth Annual Snory Awards!"

Every member of the Dreamatics hurried to sit down in the screening room, whispering excitedly. The Lunarian had not disappointed, decorating the room in trees, flowers, and birds made entirely out of pages from Luna's favorite storybooks.

The Dreamatics were all dressed in their finest finery as well. All borrowed from the costume department. This year was a literary theme: There were hungry caterpillars and mad hatters, wizards, witches, wild things, and someone wearing a giant peach.

"It's good for napping in," said Dozer from inside the fuzzy sphere.

"As you all know," said the Director, "the Snorys are an age-old tradition, awarded in all categories of dream-making. Without further ado, let's get this ceremony started."

Her introduction was followed by a glittery tap-dancing number led by Reverie, a few jokes told by members of the orchestra's woodwind section, and finally some very bad magic tricks performed by Nox and Dozer, which ended when Dozer fell asleep while being sawed in half.

"On to the awards," said the Director. "Our first Snory category is for Best Book-to-Dream Adaptation. And the award goes to . . . drumroll please . . . Nox in set design! For her work in the dream *Using a Flushing Toilet to Time Travel*. Truly gross. Truly inspiring."

Nox ran to the stage amidst raucous cheers, her eyes filling with tears as she held her award—a golden pillow-shaped trophy—high in the air.

"I just wanna thank . . . toilets, I guess," she said. "Yeah. Here's to the toilets."

The other categories were announced one by one:

THE AWARD FOR BEST SEQUEL/RECURRING DREAM:
*LUNA IS LATE FOR A CLASS SHE WAS
NEVER ENROLLED IN*

THE AWARD FOR BEST SOUND INTEGRATION:
*LUNA'S ALARM TURNS INTO A BEEPING
CHICKEN ON A FARM*

THE AWARD FOR LEAST-MEMORABLE DREAM:
*SOMETHING ABOUT A . . . TREE? A BUSH?
IT DEFINITELY HAD A PLANT IN IT . . . OR NOT*

THE AWARD FOR BEST DREAM-WITHIN-A-DREAM:
*THE FEELING OF FALLING, WAKING UP, GETTING OUT
OF BED, AND FALLING OFF THE EDGE OF THE WORLD*

The awards continued for some time—best impro-visation, weather, daydream, and so on. There was a Lifetime Achievement Award presented to the prop department—makers of fake teeth—for everyone's least-favorite recurring dream in which Luna is giving a report at school, talking to her crush, or eating a sandwich, and all her teeth fall out. Finally, we reached the lighting awards, and I crossed all my fingers and toes for Circadia.

"And the Snory for Best Lighting," said the Director, "goes to . . ."

But before the Director could say the winner's name, a giant alarm clock on the screening room wall started blaring its alert. It had always been there, but always just decorative, or so I'd thought. Lights began flashing all over the room, everyone began yelling, and life as we knew it at the Lunarian Grand came to a very abrupt, very sad end.

Chapter Nine

CODE GRIM AND MOURNFUL BLACK

"**A**HHHHHHHHHHH!!!!!"

"WHAT IS HAPPENING?!"

"WHAT DOES THAT ALARM MEAN?!"

"IS IT A FIRE? IS IT A METEOR? IS THIS PART OF THE SHOW?!"

"AHHHHHHHHHHH!!!!!"

Behind the Director the giant movie screen turned on as if we were about to watch the Daily Newsreel, but instead the words *BREAKING NEWS* flashed in red, followed by the words: *CODE LEVEL GRIM AND MOURNFUL BLACK.*

"I HAVE NO IDEA WHAT CODE LEVEL GRIM AND MOURNFUL BLACK IS," shouted a voice from the back, "BUT IT DOES NOT SOUND GOOD AT ALL!"

Everyone was in a panic but went silent when Luna and

41

her dads appeared on the screen. Below their sad faces were the words *MOMENTS AGO*. Luna was crying, and her parents seemed to be trying to explain something to her, but they kept pausing, searching for the words.

"He had a good life. A happy life, sweetheart," said Luna's father Ted.

"And he'll always be with us," said her father Matías, "in our hearts, and in our memories."

"Psst," I whispered, leaning over to Circadia. "What's a Code Grim and Mournful Black? Do you remember the theatre ever having one before?"

"Hmmm," she said, thinking. "Not that I know of, but there have been a few others. A Code Green when Luna threw up in gym class. Code Gray when her gramma Lita fell and broke her hip. But no, no Code Black. *Definitely* no Code Grim and Mournful Black. But in the world of lighting, grim and mournful means, well, something truly awful has happened. I think . . . I think it means—"

But before she could say the words, a photo of Murph the dog appeared on the screen, his tongue hanging out and tail mid-wag. His name and two dates appeared below him: one was six years ago and one...was today's date.

"My dear Dreamatics," said the Director, "a terrible accident has occurred. We've just gotten word from the Newsreel Department that Murph ran into the road and was tragically hit by a truck. It was fast, and it was pain-less, but alas . . . the curtain has drawn to a close on the life of Murph the dog."

Chapter Ten
ONE CROOKED WHISKER

I sat in silence, too stunned to move or speak. Murph . . . Murph the dog . . . *gone*? I felt like I'd lost a best friend and a piece of my own self all at once. I wanted to run away and hide in my fort to be alone, but there was more news on the screen.

Luna wanted to find a chain to wear Murph's tag from his collar around her own neck.

Luna demanded they leave Murph's bowls exactly where they were on the floor forever. Luna clung to Stan the Carrot.

Luna collected a ball of Murph's fur from the corner, sniffed it, and put it in a Ziploc bag.

And she cried.

And her fathers cried.

And the Dreamatics cried.

And I cried as well.

Eventually, Luna went to bed, but didn't sleep right away. Instead, she got out a notebook, and we watched as she made a long list. A list of every detail she could think of about Murph; everything she was afraid she might someday forget if she didn't write it down.

His one crooked whisker

His feet smell like Fritos

He looks amazing in a bandana

Mice and birds use the fur he sheds to make nests

He likes to be sung to during baths

Stinky butt (gross)

Stinky breath (strangely comforting)

Snores like rolling thunder

Hates to have his picture taken

He knows upwards of twenty words, and can, apparently, spell W–A–L–K

He's missing one permanent tooth, in the exact same place I still have a baby tooth too

The way his name tag on his collar clinks on the floor

He licks off any hand cream anyone uses, (we all have very dry skin now)

Loves to watch TV

His favorite toys (in order) are: Stan the Carrot, Gumby, Log, Log the Sequel, and Gator

Has a fluffy tail and brings nature inside stuck to it (he's a collector of sorts)

His back feet point outward like a duck

The path worn around the perimeter of the yard where he does his daily rounds

The worn couch cushion where he sleeps

The worn toys from his puppyhood that have been sewn together again and again

He has an understandable fear of the hose, (we tried to rinse mud off him once)

He has a mysterious fear of the upstairs toilet (haunted?)

The way he leaves a puddle of drool when he sleeps (they take shapes like clouds)

He once sprained his tail from wagging it too much

He's very polite

The way he groans when someone rubs his ears

He keeps a photo of his BDF (Best Dog Friend) in a little frame next to his bowls

The way he goes around the house herding everyone to bed like Nana from Peter Pan

His deep brown eyes

His joy

His lightness

His goodness

I never need a night-light as long as he is near

The way it feels to bury my head in his fur

Especially when I am heartbroken

Especially when I am sad and need to cry

Sometimes hearing his heartbeat is the only thing that can comfort me

So what do I do now, when the friend I need most is gone?

Chapter Eleven

HORN MONSTERS AND TIRE GOBLINS

Eventually the Newsreel ended, and we all stumbled back into the main theatre, too shocked to say much of anything at all. The Lunarian had changed its curtains to dark lace, and there were hundreds of candles lit all around the theatre.

"All hands on deck," said the Director. "Tonight's dream has to be perfect. In honor of Murph."

"In honor of Murph," everyone repeated, sniffling and wiping away tears.

The script was eventually delivered, and it was one of the Unseen Playwright's finest—the entire dream was written to look like a painting, with a sky in strokes of blue and the grass freshly painted green. In the dream, Luna the dreamer was able to change the color of anything and everything, making the trees purple with yellow polka dots, then plaid, then rainbow striped. It was a truly glorious dream. Or, it would have been a glorious dream, if it weren't for the dreadful Horn Monsters.

"THIS ISN'T IN THE SCRIPT!" shouted the Director. Every place the dream turned, the sound of a car's horn would blare—when the dreamer peered into a painted flower: HONK! When the dreamer looked into a painted bird's nest: HONK! When the dreamer cracked a painted book, pulled back the bed's painted blankets, opened a can of painted soup . . . the air was ravaged with HONK HONK HOOOOONK!

"It's because of the truck," I whispered to Circadia. "The one that struck Murph. The Newsreel said Luna didn't see it happen, she only heard the horrible sound of the truck's horn and screeching of tires. It's overtaking her dreams!"

And sure enough, on the second night, her dreams were overwhelmed once again.

"I'M HIDEOUS! DON'T LOOK AT ME!" shouted Reverie. The actress had been transformed into a giant, ghastly creature, shaped from rubber like a truck's tire. In the out-of-control dream, Reverie-the-Monster pulled out a large, dusty book, titled *Ghastly Spells for Tire Goblins* and began to read:

"You'll find me in my tire lair
with tire skin and tire hair
I'll turn your dreams just like a wheel

Where tires squeal and tires peal
Get ready for a nightmare ride
Nowhere to hide, nowhere to hide . . ."

"STOP! STOP EVERYTHING! THIS DREAM IS TOO SCARY!" yelled the Director. The velvet curtains crashed shut, the bead eyes now wide-open. Every Dreamatic collapsed to the floor, panting, exhausted and scared.

On the third night, Luna did not sleep. Each time the lights would dim, and the curtain would open, they would almost immediately crash shut once again. This happened all night, with the Director yelling "ACTION!" then "CUT!" until she was too hoarse to yell at all.

The next day we saw on the Newsreel that Luna was afraid to sleep, afraid of the bad dreams. Even the screening room had decorated itself to match the mood in the air—grim gray walls, talon-shaped light figures, and popcorn that tasted of hangnails and dread and expired milk.

"This is so awful," said Circadia.

"I agree," I said. "Before this, Luna's worst dream was the recurring one about the Bermuda Triangle. This is a whole other level. Makes the Bermuda Triangle Dream seem like a pretty nice vacation."

On the fourth and fifth nights, there were no dreams. We had no way to know whether Luna was awake, or in a sleeping place too deep and dark for even dreams to reach her.

On the sixth night, the show went on—the most horrible, monstrous, evil show we'd ever performed. And because Luna was so overtired at this point, even the Director couldn't get the performance to stop. The actors kept changing shape and saying lines they did not want to say.

"It's like that fairy tale Luna once read," I told Circadia. "The one where the enchanted shoes make the girl dance until she collapses."

The stage had been transformed into a haunted house, complete with strange shadows, creaking floors, and a moon shrouded in spooky clouds. Each room had some connection to Murph, and each was worse than the last. Rooms with serpents made from dog leashes, rooms with squeak toy zombies, and rooms with dancing skeletons made from dog treat bones. In the last dream before she woke, Luna found the Hairwolf, a pile of dog hair that turned into a werewolf with the full moon. The last sound of the night was its dreadful howl.

"This can't go on," said the Director, visibly shaken. "Something has got to change."

And, luckily, something did: On the seventh night the Unseen Playwright wrote a dream starring Murph the dog. It was odd, though—the dream wasn't delivered by the script shooting through the Pipe Dream and landing in the Director's hands. It came in like a secret, like a wish, slipped inside a book prop during one of Luna's nightmares.

"No matter how it came," said the Director, "this is just what Luna needs—to see Murph again in her dreams. It will surely lift her spirits, like a good memory, or a favorite song."

But when the time came for the performance, and Reverie was supposed to morph into Murph the dog, she stayed in her own Reverie form.

She furrowed her brow, and tried again.

And again.

And again.

But it was no use.

It seemed that Murph the dog was not only gone from the real world; he was gone from the dream world as well.

Chapter Twelve

WORRYWORTS, ANXIEFLEAS, AND FRETLETTES

As if things weren't awful enough with all the nightmares, the Lunarian Grand had also become infested with irritants. It was awash in annoyances. We were plagued by pestering pests. They slept in our teacups, bathed in our soup bowls, and chewed holes through every last costume, hat, and shoe.

"We can only perform shows where everyone plays Swiss cheese now!" cried Tuck, holding up a dress full of holes.

Elsewhere, Circadia struggled with chewed-through wires, Dozer was awakened from every nap by the pitter-patter of wee feet, and the orchestra found nests in every cello, trumpet, and tuba.

"What we're dealing with here," said the Director, "are Worryworts."

"Worryworts?" everyone asked.

"Exactly," continued the Director. "Worryworts, Anxiefleas, and Fretlettes. The trauma of Murph's untimely passing must have caused strain on the structural integrity of the Lunarian Grand, which caused the cracks that these pests use to get inside. And now . . . we're infested."

"Ew. Can't we, like, put out traps or something?" asked Reverie.

"They're far too smart for that," said the Director. "They chew away at the walls, the floors, the ceilings. They can chew out entire doorways . . . doorways to let in . . . well, we don't speak of that. Of them."

"Them?" cried Winks the conductor. "Them *who?!* Oh, the horror. The HORROR!"

But the Director either didn't hear or didn't want to answer the question, because she instead looked at her watch and started walking toward the screening room. Not knowing what else to do, we all followed her to watch the Daily Newsreel.

"Ack!" we heard the Director shout as we rushed into the room behind her.

"They're so . . . fluffy," said Circadia.

"And there's so many of them," said Tuck.

"Worryworts," said the Director.

They were referring to the furball creatures—each spherical and no bigger than a kitten—that were sitting in every viewing seat in the screening room. They were sipping soft drinks, eating candy and popcorn, and seemed to be waiting for the show.

"Hey! Get outta here!" yelled Nox.

The Worryworts' fur was colored blue at first, but when Nox started yelling at them, the fur changed to a deep green, then purple, then angry orange.

"They're like mood rings!" said Tuck. "Mood rings that bite!"

"Go on, ya varmints," said Nox, shooing them out of the door and closing it behind them.

Once the room was cleared of Worryworts, we brushed the fur from our seats and sat down as the Daily Newsreel began. And what did we find there?

Horror, as Winks would say. Nothing but HORROR.

Or at least horror for a Dream Theatre like us.

"I'm not going to sleep anymore," Luna announced to her dads over breakfast.

"Oh?"

"Yeah," continued Luna, "I've decided it's just not for me."

"I don't think that's the best idea," said her father Ted, sipping his tea. "Sleep deprivation can lead to high blood pressure, diabetes, depression, and reduced immune system function."

"I'm ten," said Luna. "How high can my blood pressure possibly get?"

She took a heaping spoonful of sugar from the dish and added it to her cereal.

"Sugar," she said, "keeps you awake."

"That's a sugar substitute," said her dad.

"THIS FAMILY IS TOO HEALTHY," groaned Luna.

It was a Saturday, which was when Luna's family usually went to the library, but Luna told her dads that libraries are peaceful and quiet and cozy, and those are things she no longer welcomed in her life.

Instead, she started her day with a horror film, one with giant people-eating plants. She only made it halfway through before her dad found her watching it and made her turn it off.

"It's rated PG!" said Luna.

"Parental," said her dad, pointing to himself, "guidance."

After doing her homework while blaring loud music, eating a lunch and dinner that Luna requested include lots of sugary fruits, and taking a cold shower instead of her usual warm bath, Luna's dads insisted she get into bed.

"If you have a bad dream, we're right down the hall," said her dad. "Just come wake us up. We love you very much."

"I won't have to wake you up," said Luna, "because I'm not going to sleep."

Her dad shut off all her lights except her night-light, blew her a kiss, and closed the door.

And that's when the real horror movie began. Normally, this was the time when we would be performing, but instead we'd set up Command Central in the screening room, everyone waiting and watching to see if Luna was ever going to fall asleep.

"Where are we at, team?" asked the Director, standing with a headset like mission control at NASA during a rocket launch.

"She's cranked up the air conditioner to full blast," reported Tuck. "She's wearing a winter coat inside."

"Lighting status?"

"All on full brightness," reported Circadia. "And she gathered some lamps from around the house, and those are all on too. Highest wattage bulbs she could find. It's like the surface of the sun in there, team. Nobody could sleep in these conditions."

We watched Luna work out to one of her dad's old exercise tapes—something called Jazzercize—to keep herself occupied. She tried acupressure points on her hand that claimed to promote wakefulness, pinched herself about a million times, and even went out onto the deck in the rain to stay awake.

It was working too—it was nearly dawn and the Dreamatics Mission Control team was rumpled and sweaty, with wadded-up papers from failed ideas and empty coffee cups covering every surface. Everyone was ready to call it quits when a loud POP! came from the Newsreel and jolted us to attention.

"Houston, we have a problem!" yelled the Director.

On-screen, Luna's dads rushed into her room in their

pajamas, frantic with worry. But all they found was Luna, her floor covered in blown-up balloons, popping them one by one.

"Loud noises," she said, "help you stay awake."

Luna's dads looked at each other helplessly.

The Dreamatics all looked at one another hopelessly.

In reply there came a deafening POP! POP! POP! as Luna burst every balloon.

Chapter Thirteen
THE DEPARTMENT OF FORGOTTEN THINGS

After our troubling night in the screening room, I made my way back to prop storage and my fort made of sand. I needed some time to think, to process everything that was happening. But when I settled down inside, I noticed several of my trinkets were missing from the shelves—I searched but couldn't find the first-leaf-to-fall from a dream last autumn, the shark tooth Luna bought at the aquarium and put on a necklace, or the fairy wing she once dreamed she'd found in a forest.

"Hey! Stop!" I shouted as several balls of fur scurried away carrying one of my favorite seashells. The Worryworts were colored a shade of yellow, but as I yelled at them, they turned a deep, anxious red.

"Get back here, thieves!"

I tried to catch the fluff balls, but they slipped out a tunnel they'd burrowed in the sand wall. I leaped up and out of my fort in hot pursuit. I followed them out of set storage and down the hallway maze, and finally to the open door of a large room I'd never noticed before. The sign over the door read: *DEPARTMENT OF FORGOTTEN THINGS*.

Strange, I thought, *I don't remember ever hearing about this place.*

The large room was actually several rooms, all connected like the exhibits in a museum. The first area had a sign that read *WISHES*, and in the display cases were coins Luna had thrown into fountains, jars of dandelion seeds, floating replicas of stars she'd made wishes on, and even a display of melted candles from all her birthday cake wishes from past years.

The next section, labeled *LUNAZOOLOGY*, contained long rows of glass cases, just like the dioramas of taxidermy animals in natural history museums. But these creatures weren't exactly natural. The first one was at least ten feet tall, striped and polka-dotted in every color imaginable, with eight eyes and a daffodil growing from its head. I looked to the side of the diorama and there was a framed crayon drawing with a label that said *LUNA, AGE 4, DAFFODRAGON*.

"Hey, I remember that drawing," I mumbled to myself.

The Daffodragon moved, eating the grass and smiling. I wondered if this was robotics or holograms or . . .

magic? The other dioramas held similar creatures from Luna's imaginative artwork and dreams: a spikey-haired cactus pig called *SPINEYSWINEY*, tree-sized trolls called *OAKOFOLD*, and a glowing unicorn. *LUNA, AGE 6, RAZZMATAZZACORN*, read the sign. The Razzmatazzacorn looked at me, sighed heavily, then sneezed out a spray of glitter.

"Ick!" I said, jumping back. The glass in front of me was covered in wet sparkles. "Who knew glitter could be so gross?"

The next room was less active, but just as beautiful, and labeled *BOTTLES OF SCENTS ROOM*. The walls were lined with shelves that held endless glass bottles. Each had a little tag attached with a description: *ESSENCE OF ART CLASS, ESSENCE OF PUBLIC POOL, ESSENCE OF KITTEN*. I picked up one labeled *ESSENCE OF MONKEY BARS*, unstopped the cork, and sniffed.

"Smells like . . . hands after they've been swinging on a metal jungle gym and . . . freshly cut grass and . . ." I took another sniff. ". . . laughter."

I heard a SMASH! from behind me and turned to see that the Worryworts had caused a bottle to fall to the ground and break, the spilled liquid evaporating into a swirl of orange smoke that smelled of love, a parade, and mashed potatoes. I picked up the shard that had a tag attached.

"'*ESSENCE OF THANKSGIVING DINNER,*'" I read. "Well that's just great, you stinking varmints. We could have used this! Maybe! For . . . whatever these are used for . . ."

The Worryworts were on the move once again, so I quickly grabbed a bottle that was teetering on the edge of a shelf called *ESSENCE OF MURPH*, threw it in my pocket, and gave chase. They led me through corridors and rooms, up stairs, down stairs, and into places I'd never ventured. When I couldn't run any longer, I stopped to catch my breath outside a stairwell that only went down, not up. I assumed it was some sort of basement, maybe where the Worryworts, Anxiefleas, and Fretlettes had their nest. I started down the stairs, down, down, down, finally reaching a door in the very darkest corner. It was stark white, in contrast to the shadowy depths, and had a sign that read:

SUBCONSCIOUS FLOOR
UNCONSCIOUS FUNCTIONS, GUT INSTINCTS,
BELIEFS, SLEEP

Sleep? I wondered. *What was a sleep department doing down here? Wasn't that what we did up in the theatre?* Below the official department label, there was a Post-it with a note on it. It read:

OUT
FOR
~~COFFEE~~ *Ever*

To be honest, I wasn't sure if I was authorized to see any of the things inside this department, so I decided to leave the decision up to the door. But when I turned the knob, it was unlocked. I had no idea I was about to come face-to-face with the mysterious, the possibly dangerous, the never-before-seen . . . Unseen Playwright.

Chapter Fourteen

THE SELF-TYPING TYPEWRITER

Well, *almost* face-to-face.

When I stepped inside the office, it appeared I'd just missed the Unseen Playwright by mere seconds—a mug of tea still had steam coming off the top, and a spoon was self-stirring inside. Beside it was a muffin with one bite taken out of it, and a very large, old-fashioned typewriter. The typewriter had a piece of paper hanging over the back, and on it was half a page of dialogue and stage direction for a new dream.

I moved closer, my eyes hovering over the words to try to read them, when ZIP! CLANG! The typewriter carriage moved on its own back to the left and started a new sentence. I watched as the keys to various letters were pressed as if by invisible ghost fingers, and read as it typed "%$&*%@ ODIUHFGDHGIEO HELP HELP HELP HELP HELP HELP GHEIOQWVBN@#*$."

I jumped back. "Sorry," I said, feeling like I'd somehow scared the typewriter. *Great,* I thought, *now I'm apologizing to office appliances.* Although . . . maybe it wasn't actually afraid of me. Maybe it was asking me for help. But why would a typewriter need help?

"Hello?" I said tentatively. The keyboard had the normal buttons like letters, numbers, punctuation. But there were others as well, ones that read DAD, PAPA, LITA (Luna's grandmother), OLIVER and OLIVIA (twins that lived on Luna's street), CHEWGUM (Luna's [former] imaginary friend), and VONSCREECH (the ghost that probably lived in Luna's attic). These must be characters recurrent enough in Luna's dreams to get their own buttons. There was another key beside the caps lock that said PUNCT+, and when I pressed it, all the keys turned to punctuation marks I'd never seen before—swirls, starbursts, teardrops, and more—and each had a fancy word like ENNUI, HIRAETH, and DÉJÀ VU. I pressed the key that felt the most fitting, a swirling scribble that said CONFUDDLED, but the key had hardly hit the paper before the typewriter started typing madly. "%$&*%@ ODI-UHFGDHGIEO YES CONFUDDLED CONFUSED ALONE LOST ALONE HELP HELP HELP GHEIOQWVBN@#*$."

I jumped back, then leaned in slowly to reread the odd words. *Had something . . . bad happened to the Unseen Playwright?* I wondered. *Was that who needed help?*

It was time to investigate.

I read the spines of the books on the Playwright's

desk, titles like *The Encyclopedia of Magical Dream Creatures, Growing Your Dream Garden, Dream Ingredients, An Actor's Guide to Transfiguration, Under the Pillow: Behind the Dream Scene,* and *The Dreaming Book of Dreams.* I picked up the last, opened to a random page, and immediately heard a muffled voice that seemed to come from the depths of the book's crease shout, "Oy! Shut the cover, I'm trying to sleep here."

I dropped the book and investigated the large machinery around the room, some covered in dust cloths. I pulled off the cloths one by one, studying each contraption, trying to make sense of what I was seeing. The first machine looked like a roulette wheel, with just about every possible noun written on it. When I reached out and gave it a spin, the words changed, each one rearranging its letters into more possibilities. While it spun, however, several pieces fell off, and words began collecting in a pile around my feet—words like *BEACH* and *FIREFLY* and *SNOW DAY.* I saw there were already piles of words in every corner, raked up like leaves in the fall. I picked up a few from the top of the closest pile, and read: *CAMP, HALLOWEEN, BOOKSHOP, DONUTS, THE OCEAN, HONEY, COWS, TOADSTOOLS, MURPH.*

"Murph?" I said. "What are you doing in this pile?" I put the word in my overall pocket. It seemed wrong to leave Murph's name on the floor. I added a few of the other words as well, to keep Murph's company.

After the words had fallen off, I looked back at the

roulette wheel and read the ones that remained: *POISON IVY, VONSCREECH, GHOUL, BASEMENT, FLU, ZOMBIES.*

I shuddered.

The other machines were similar to the roulette wheel. There was a dart game with only words like *SNOT, SLUG-SLIME,* and *MOLD* left up on the dartboard; a ball toss like at the carnival with goldfish, but only words like *SORROWFUL, GLOOMY,* and *SAD* were left swimming in the bowls. On the far end of the room was a cupboard, and inside were endless wee tightly rolled fortune-telling scrolls in every color. I tried opening a few, and lo and behold, each one was worse than the last.

"You will be chased by a giant centipede," I read. "You will be shipwrecked in the Bermuda Triangle with killer centipedes," said the next. "You will be turned into a centipede."

"Who wrote these?" I asked. "A centipede?"

I guessed that the machines and fortune scrolls helped the Unseen Playwright write Luna's dreams—whichever words or prompts he came upon became the subjects of Luna's dream scripts. But clearly all the machines were malfunctioning—the roulette wheel had lost all its happy words, the dartboard and ball toss had only bleak choices, and the scrolls were telling only centipede-related fortunes.

But worst of all, there was no Unseen Playwright to fix it.

Is this the end? I wondered. *Is Luna doomed to have bad dreams . . . forever?*

The plot seemed clear: I needed to find the Unseen Playwright so he could write a new dream. But that plan was awful because, duh, the Playwright was *Unseen*. As in impossible to find. And also . . . missing? Get a clue, Dormir.

As I was busy belittling myself, a new idea—possibly more awful than the first—snuck its sneaky way into my mind.

Maybe there's a way to do what the missing Playwright and his broken machines can't, said the idea.

Maybe, just maybe, you could craft something new, something better, something that would make Luna feel less helpless, lost, and alone, whispered the thought.

Could I do it? I wondered. *Could I, lowlier-than-low assistant Dormir, write a new dream?*

Chapter Fifteen
WORST REGARDS

My feet couldn't carry me fast enough back up the stairs and through the twist of hallways. The only thing that kept running through my mind was *We must, we must, we must find a way to put these good things back into Luna's dreams.* Forget the Unseen Playwright! We'd write them ourselves, we'd . . . *Hey, I don't remember ever being here before,* I thought, entering the Department of Forgotten Things. No time to stop and look, though I did catch a few glimpses as I raced past shelves of bottles, coins, candles, stars, creatures, and one . . . glitter-sneezing unicorn?

While I rushed back to the theatre, I tried thinking of a good story for the dream I would write for Luna. I took out the happy words I'd put into my pocket and read through them: *MURPH, SINGING, FRESH LAUNDRY, MARSHMALLOWS, SEQUINS, SWEATERS, HOME.* Maybe I could write a dream where Murph was dressed in a sequin sweater and singing a song? No, that didn't sound like Murph's style at all. Maybe one where Murph was a giant marshmallow, and was larger than the house? And . . . doing the laundry? No, no, no. That was even worse than the first idea! Maybe this was going to be harder than I'd thought . . .

I must have gotten turned around somewhere in the labyrinth of the theatre—either that or I'd entered a cunning corridor or perfidious passageway—because instead of arriving at the stage I ended up in the lobby next to the concession stand, with its magical candies and fizzy drinks fountain, and in front of the double doors that opened into the theatre. I looked for Dozer near the marquee to tell him my news, but he was nowhere to be found. And where was everyone else? Why was it so eerily quiet? And why were the doors closed? They were never closed, except during a performance.

I pulled the door handle to go inside, but it didn't budge. I tried the other door, and it was stuck as well.

"How odd . . ." I said.

I was about to knock and make a ruckus, when in front of me appeared a sign, written in perfect calligraphy on white parchment. The letters were too faint to read at first but slowly came into focus, as if the ink was given power and depth by the very act of being read.

THEATRE UNDER NEW MANAGEMENT.
WORST REGARDS,
THE BAD DREAMS

Chapter Sixteen

COCO AND THE BAD DREAMS

Since the door was locked, I leaned down, closed one eye, and peered through the keyhole. Once my vision focused, I saw the truth: The Lunarian Grand looked *awful*—sickly, depressed, and unbathed. The curtains around the stage had started to mold and decay, and the beaded eyes were open but red-rimmed and bloodshot. The velvet chairs were stained and ripped, springs showing like skeleton bones. Even the two statues that flanked the top corners of the stage had become gargoyle-like, covered in vines and dead leaves. When one of them reared back and yell-sneezed "AAAA-CHOO!" before letting out a hacking cough, it vibrated all the way across the theatre and I felt a jolt of panic; the Lunarian Grand was ill from its highest beams to its haunted basement, and its light was dying away.

Suddenly, the doors to the theatre opened, and I

tumbled forward onto the stinky boots of a stranger.

"Oy, what are you doing loitering out here? You better have a ticket to the show and not be trying to sneak on in."

I was pulled up by my overalls to face a towering, cobweb-covered stranger carrying a clipboard and letters for the marquee. His skin was a purplish greenish gray like an old bruise, covered in warts and scars.

"T-ticket?" I said, my voice shaking. "I don't need a ticket, I work here."

"I don't think so," said the creature. "I'm good at re-membering faces, and I'm getting nothing from yours. It's like looking at a potato. A loaf of bread. A doorknob."

"Well, who are you?" I asked, trying to gather up any scraps of courage.

"*I* work here," said the creature. "For Coco."

I furrowed my brow in confusion. "That name . . . it sounds so familiar . . ."

"Coco!" said the creature, more emphatically. "Of Coco and the Bad Dreams?!" He said this like they were the Beatles and Elvis and Beyoncé together on tour. "Ugh, *someone's* behind the times. Just follow me."

We entered the theatre and I looked around for a familiar face, but there was none to be found—only strangers, the smell of mildew and mothballs, and a the-atre in distress. In the Director's chair sat an even larger creature with its back to us, and as we got closer, I saw that it had squeezed itself into a T-shirt with a donut design on the back and the words *DONUT STRESS ME OUT*.

"Hey!" I said. "That's not your ridiculous shirt! That's the Director's ridiculous shirt."

The creature turned slowly, like a movie villain, and I gasped. In his lap sat the largest Worrywort I'd seen, colored a joyless gray and wearing a gold tag that read *Nighmeria*. That was not why I'd gasped, however. It was because the creature holding the Worrywort was someone indescribably scary. *Literally* indescribable. As I looked at him, he came in and out of focus like a trick to the eye, like heat off hot pavement. One minute he had rotten candy corn teeth and skin like a bubbling cauldron, then the next fangs like brittle branches, eyes like a swampy marsh, and a comb-over of cobwebs for hair. He seemed to be able to change shape differently from any Dreamatic I'd seen—it was as if his entire being was made up of nightmares and dark shadows.

"Ah, you must be Dormir," he said, his voice like a rusty swing set creaking in the wind. "Those Dream-misfits were wondering where you were before they all ran off. Here to beg for a job?"

He seemed so familiar, like a memory, or a bad idea, or . . . a story.

And then it hit me: *I knew Coco.*

I'd always known him.

And so had Luna.

"Coco," I said, trying to keep my voice steady. "Like Luna's Lita used to tell spooky bedtime stories about?

But you're not real. . . . You're just a character in a lullaby meant to scare kids so they'll behave and go to sleep."

"Oh, really?" said Coco, standing up and coming closer, his scent of slug slime and minnow's breath swirling around me. "I *feel* like I'm real. Don't I *look* like I'm real?"

He started humming Lita's lullaby: *Duérmete niño, duérmete . . . Sleep child, sleep now, else Coco will come and will eat you.* When Coco reached out a murky finger and tapped me on the nose, I jolted upright, as if I'd just awakened from a particularly horrifying nightmare, my body covered in sweat, my skin crawling like mice in the walls.

"I'm as real," he continued, "as my brothers the Oogly Boogly and the Bogeyman. As real as my great-auntie Baba Yaga. As my cousins twice removed, the Monster in the Closet, the Creature Under the Bed, and the Thing That Goes Bump in the Night."

"Okay, so you're real," I said, "but where did you come from? What are you doing *here*?"

"We're the Bad Dreams, from the Wrong Side of the Bed, and we'll be taking over the performances here at the Lunarian Grand from now on. Every. Single. Night. Ah, look," said Coco, motioning toward the crumbling stage. "A new nightmare is about to be performed. And *I'm* the star. Won't you stay and enjoy the show?"

Chapter Seventeen
AHHHHHHH!!!

This chapter is too scary!
Save yourself!
Stop reading!
Why are you still reading?!
Put the book down!
I beg of you . . .

Chapter Eighteen

THE GUILT TRIP

Onstage, a nightmare is unfolding.

The Bad Dreams lighting department has somehow managed to perfectly re-create the light in Luna's bedroom when it's the dead of winter and there's a full moon outside. It's an eerie light, making it just bright enough in the room that everything—from the puppet theatre to a pile of clothes on a chair—looks like a swamp monster in the shadows. The only thing out of place is a suitcase in the corner. It's Luna's, but it usually stays stored in the attic, not sprawled on her floor. And it definitely doesn't open by itself, which is exactly what it is doing right now.

As the suitcase creaks open like a door in a haunted house, the smell of slug slime and minnow's breath fills the theatre, along with notes of mildew and fresh dirt. It is the smell of Coco. He emerges from the suitcase, but has transformed perfectly into the shape of Luna, from her dark ponytail to her braces. The only thing wrong is her eyes, which are smoke-filled and dark like Coco himself.

The air in the theatre becomes stifling and damp, like being tangled in bedsheets during a nightmare. Coco-Luna creeps over squeaking floorboards to the bed, where a person-shaped lump is under blankets, fast asleep, and he begins shaking the lump, his voice a funhouse-version of Luna's. "Wake up, Luna! Wake up! Don't you see that Murph has to go potty? How can you just ignore him? How can you be so lazy, so cruel? You never spent enough time with him. And now it's too late."

Suddenly, the stage fogs over and changes, the set now Luna's front yard, still covered in frozen snow, still lit only by the moon. Coco-Luna is kneeling, frantically digging through the same suitcase, screaming, "No, no, noooo! I need to lock the gate! If I don't lock the gate, he'll get out. He'll run into the road . . ." The suitcase is crammed with keys of every shape and size. They have legs and antennae and scuttle away like insects. "None of these Lockcrawlers is right, none of them will ever reach the gate in time."

The final act is in a courthouse, vast and endless and so cold, the seats in the theatre chatter like teeth. Coco-Luna sits in the judge's seat, with a jury of dead-eyed strangers in the jury box.

"And how do you judge one Luna Grande?" asks Coco. "Charged with being at fault for the death of one Murph the dog?"

One of the jurors stands and opens the same suitcase.

From inside she pulls a scroll of paper, unfurls it, and screams the verdict.

"GUILTY.

"GUILTY.

"GUILTY!"

Chapter Nineteen
THE BEST LAST DAY

"Well, that was . . . alarming," I said to myself as I crept to the back of the theatre and tiptoed up the steps to Circadia's lighting department. There was glass on the floor from broken bulbs, and cords and wires were tied in un-untangleable knots.

"Pssst," I said into the darkness. "Bug-Eyes, this is Lowly Nobody, are you in here?"

"Are those our code names?" said Circadia, peeking out from behind a stack of cardboard boxes. "Do these make me look like a bug?" she asked, touching her glasses. "I love bugs."

"The theatre is overrun with bogies and goblins and ghouls!" I yell-whispered.

"I'm aware," said Circadia. "Coco came and . . ." She motioned to the broken glass in rainbow shards at her feet. ". . . said hello."

"Circadia! Whaterwegonnado?" I squeaked.

"Well, I just finished lovingly packing away the lighting fixtures that weren't destroyed. And by my watch," she continued, "it's about time for the Daily Newsreel. So, we should probably make our way over to the screening room."

"But . . . how . . . and what . . . and they . . ." I sputtered, following behind her. "And you . . . what about . . . and then . . . how could . . . disaster . . ."

Once we reached the screening room, we found several interesting things. The first was that there *was* in fact a Daily Newsreel, and it was just beginning to play on-screen. The second was that the screening room had redecorated itself once again, the theme now apparently "Swamp Chic," with a gurgling bog covering most of the floor, dead tree roots, and the smell of sulfur filling the air.

"How cozy," said Circadia, climbing over the seats to avoid the mess. "Oh, pardon me, sir. Wait, Dozer? Is that you? I thought all the other Dreamatics were gone!"

"Huh, what?" said Dozer, waking and rubbing his eyes. "Why would everyone be gone? I was dreaming of alligators and rotten eggs . . ."

"Don't worry about it, buddy," she said, patting his head as he drifted back to sleep. "It's really good to see you, though."

I joined Circadia, and we perched together on the backs of our seats like vultures. We held hands, unsure what was to come. On the screen, Luna appeared, seated across from an older woman I'd never seen before.

"So, Luna," said the woman, "your dads tell me you've been feeling a lot of guilt. Maybe we can try to unpack that together."

Luna went wide-eyed and gripped the sides of her chair. "Doctor Dawn, would that involve . . . a suitcase?" she asked.

Dr. Dawn gave Luna a warm smile. "No literal suitcases, just talking. Luna, you've recently gone through a traumatic experience, and there's no right or wrong way to feel. It can be very lonely. I want you to know there's no judgment here about any of the things we talk about. With that in mind, why do you think you're here?"

"Um . . ." said Luna, "I guess because I've been having trouble sleeping. And when I do, I just have nightmares. And . . ."

"Take your time," said Dr. Dawn.

"And because it's my fault," whispered Luna. "It was just a regular day, and I wasn't paying attention to him. I never paid enough attention to him. If I had just known . . ."

"If you had known?" asked Dr. Dawn.

"If I had known it was our last day together," said Luna, "I would have done everything."

"Everything?"

"Everything that Murph loved. I'd have my dad take us for a last ride in the truck so Murph could put his head out the window and feel the wind blowing in his face, ears flying. We'd drive by the house where Murph's BDF lives. That's Best Dog Friend," explained Luna. "And they would chase each other around the yard like hands on a clock. At home we'd pull out photo albums, and look at pictures of us growing up, and laugh at our worst haircuts through the years. Murph and I would talk about the things we'd always talked about together, his secrets and mine. We'd eat all the forbidden foods Murph always wanted—especially bacon. So much bacon. Bouquets of bacon tied up with ribbons." Luna's eyes prickled with tears, and she smiled at the thought. "We'd sleep nose to nose all night, and in the early morning, he'd take his time around the perimeter of the dewy garden, as if he realized this was his last pre-dawn patrol, his last chance to scare every frog into the pond. He'd try to eat a pale blue hydrangea bloom, like always, and I'd think to myself, *I'll remember this every year when they bloom.* We'd take our last *W-A-L-K* and he'd leave his mark on every familiar bush and mailbox. I'd make sure he had The Best Last Day."

"The Best Last Day," repeated Dr. Dawn.

"And at the end of it," said Luna, "I'd whisper in his ear."

"What would you say?"

"I'd say . . . *every day with you was the best day.*"

80

Chapter Twenty
THE OVERLY TALKATIVE TEAKETTLE

There weren't seasons at the Lunarian Grand, not exactly—more like emotional climates, (unless you count the frequent hijinks spilling from the weather closet). After the Bad Dreams took over, the theatre plunged into the slow decay of late autumn—chilly crow-caw air, the smell of dying leaves, and a general sense of spookiness.

"My hope," I said to Circadia and a dozing Dozer as we sat in my sandcastle fort, "is that the changes in the atmosphere are just the Lunarian's maudlin reaction to the Bad Dreams and not . . . you know . . . the actual slow death of the theatre."

"Also," said Circadia, "the fireplace isn't working."

I'd invited them over to tell them about my discoveries and to hopefully come up with a plan together. Normally, when there was a shiver in the air, the Lunarian would light me a cozy fire in my fort. But this time, no such enchantment or luck.

"Do you think the Lunarian is—"

"Don't say it," I said, cutting Circadia off.

"—losing its magic?" she continued anyway.

We made do with lighting several pillar candles in the unlit fireplace and heating water for tea in a teakettle. I was always discovering new oddities in prop storage, and this teakettle was one such item. It boiled hot water whenever asked, sure, but instead of giving a whistle when it was ready, it instead shrieked never-ending factoids.

"AND THE THING ABOUT BEES," screamed the kettle in its high-pitched whistle, "IS THAT THEY COMMUNICATE WITH ONE ANOTHER BY DANCING. ONE-THIRD OF THE FOOD HUMANS EAT IS THE RESULT OF HONEYBEE POLLINATION. HONEY HAS BEEN FOUND THAT'S TWO THOUSAND YEARS OLD AND IT TASTES—"

But the kettle had run out of steam.

Other Dreamatics had their own charmed teakettles, but they all seemed superior to mine—a Foresee Pot that revealed fortunes, a Quip 'n' Sip that told jokes, and the Fondue 'n' Brew that was . . . always filled with hot cheese. Okay, maybe I had the *second*-worst teakettle in the theatre.

"Listen . . . I have to tell you something," I said, knowing I couldn't delay sharing my bad news any longer. "The Unseen Playwright is gone. I went to the Sub Floor, and all I found were malfunctioning dream-writing machines, a haunted typewriter, and *this*."

I held up the muffin I'd stolen from the Unseen Playwright's office. It was slightly less dramatic than I'd intended, but Circadia and Dozer did look properly shocked by my news.

"I briefly thought I could write some new dreams for Luna until the Unseen Playwright came back," I confessed, "but that was before I knew about the Bad Dreams. Do we have any ideas what to do about them?"

"One way to not have bad dreams," said Circadia, "could be to not have any dreams at all. So, what about Insomnia?" asked Circadia.

"DON'T SAY THAT," yell-whispered Dozer, looking around as if he'd seen a ghost. "You could summon her."

Insomnia was a much-speculated-about but clearly unreal specter of the theatre.

"We can summon Insomnia?" asked Circadia.

Dozer gasped. "STOP SAYING HER NAME!"

"Whose name?" asked Circadia. "Insomnia's?"

"Well, you've gone and done it now," said Dozer. "You said Insomnia's name three times!"

"Four if you count the one you just said," said Circadia. "Ooooh, does that qualify us for a bonus haunting?"

"THE LETTERS IN *SCUBA* STAND FOR *SELF-CONTAINED UNDERWATER BREATHING APPARATUS*," interrupted the kettle, which had reached boiling once again and was yelling about acronyms. *"ASAP* STANDS FOR *AS SOON AS POSSIBLE. DREAM* STANDS FOR *DRAMATIC RE-ENACTMENTS OF ACCLAIMED MEMO-RIES . . ."*

I turned to Dozer and Circadia. "Whoa, did you hear what the kettle just screamed?"

"I agree," said Circadia. *"Scuba* is a very fun word. Scooooooba. ScooOOOoooba."

"No," I said, "the part about the word dream. Did you know it stands for . . . what'd it say?"

"Dramatic Re-Enactments of Acclaimed Memories," said Circadia. "Yeah, I thought everyone knew that."

"Well, I didn't!" I said, a bit too loudly. "Because if I had, I might have realized that could be the answer. *Memories.*"

"Memories?" asked Circadia and Dozer.

"Reverie can't turn into Murph anymore, right?" I continued. "So Murph isn't in Luna's dreams. But what if we went and found a *memory* of Murph. We could take the Murph out of the memory and put him into a dream. Luna would see him again and be happy. The Bad Dreams would have to leave!"

"It's a great plan," said Circadia. "Top-notch stuff."

"Thank you," I said, beaming.

"Only one problem," she continued. She pretended to look around the fort. She lifted up several trinkets and seashells and looked beneath them. She gazed into the bottom of her empty teacup. "I don't see any memories just lying around. Do you?"

"No . . ." I said. I knew Circadia was just trying to help, but I felt deflated.

"And I don't think any of us have any idea where to find one."

"*PERHAPS I COULD LEND A HELPING HAAAAAAND,*" boomed a deep, menacing voice from outside the fort.

A black cape flashed over the doorway like a thundercloud.

The voice cackled laughter like lightning.

And we all screamed in unison at the horror darkening our doorway.

Chapter Twenty-one
LE SABOTEUR

"**W**inks?!" we all said together, once we'd finished our screaming and realized the cape-clad figure was actually our conductor.

"What are you doing here?" I asked. "I thought you fled the theatre with the others."

"Fled? Me? Do I *seem* like the kind of individual who's so overly dramatic that I would FLEE FROM DANGER?"

Circadia and I gave each other a sideways glance, wondering if we should answer.

"I sent my orchestra away, to the farthest reaches of this twisted, winding theatre. But I…" said Winks, a hand to his heart, "I stayed. I shall go down with this ship. I shall descend with this playhouse like a leading lady through a trapdoor. I shall collapse with it like a middle school production of *Les Misérables*. I shall—"

"Winks!" I shouted. "What did you mean when you said you could lend us a helping hand? Do you know where to find a memory?"

"Ah yes! The Memory Bank," he said, "on Memory Lane."

"What's the Memory Bank?" I asked.

"As you may know," said Winks, "some theatres have trapdoors, ones that lead to a recess beneath the stage. And there are many types of trapdoors—cauldron trapdoors where things are passed up, or star trapdoors where actors are propelled from below. And then there's the grave trap. What a name! And this is used to lower an actor from the stage to whatever lies below . . . and is also the kind of trapdoor that we have here in the Lunarian Grand."

"We have a trapdoor?" said Circadia. "Awesome. Where does it lead, to a creepy basement? Australia? The *underworld*?"

"Ah, that's the mystery," continued Winks. "But gossip says that it leads to other areas of Luna's cerebral imaginatory wonderland, if you will. Rumor has it, that trapdoor leads to Memory Lane, home of the Memory Bank."

"This . . . this is amazing . . ." I said, pacing the floor. "This is what we were looking for. Let's go down the trapdoor right now!"

"Not so fast," said Winks. "The door is definitively, undeniably, absolutely, unquestionably, and emphatically. . . locked. And there is no key. HOWEVER, hope lives on. I have it on good authority that Coco is in possession of one Lockcrawler prop he captured from Luna's suitcase nightmare. Which could open the door."

"Okay," said Circadia, pushing up her glasses. "I'll do it. I'll fight him to the death."

"Violence is not necessary, little one," said Winks, "as I have a plan. Dozer, you monitor the screening room. Dormir and Circadia, you'll go to the stage and idle near Coco. Meanwhile, *Le Saboteur* will—"

"Wait," interrupted Circadia. "Who is *Le Saboteur*?"

"I am," said Winks, exasperated. "Obviously. Don't you see my blacker-than-usual cape? My velvet gloves? My spooky masquerade mask, which is in my pocket, because it was irritating my eyes and sensitive skin?"

We gave him drowning looks of impatience.

"Sorry, sorry," he continued. "As I was saying, I'll distract Coco, and you two can grab the Lockcrawler, open the lock, and scurry down the trapdoor."

"That sounds"—I gulped—"dangerous."

"Not for . . ." said Winks, backing away while doing jazz hands, ". . . *Le Saboteur!*"

✳   ✳   ✳

When Circadia and I reached the theatre, we found that things had changed once again. The theatre seats had turned gray, looking more like gravestones, and there were spots of moss, mold, and lichen over just about every surface.

But worst of all, the infestation had reached epic proportions, and Worryworts, Anxiefleas, and Fretlettes covered the entire theatre—they were sitting in every open seat in the audience, eating popcorn and candy; they had made nests out of costume thread, prop hats, and lighting cords; and a line of them seemed to be doing a choo-choo train dance down the center aisle.

"Well, at least they're having fun," said Circadia, her voice thick with sarcasm.

"Look," I said, pointing, "there he is."

Onstage, surrounded by his minions, sat Coco in a throne-like chair made from welded-together Snory Awards and Nighmeria on his lap. The ginormous Worrywort seemed to have grown even larger, and was batting something between its paws.

"What's it got there?" I whispered. "A mouse?" We crept through the shadows along the walls of the theatre, making our way up the stairs to the stage and behind some boxes. We were close enough to smell Coco's stale cheese breath and read his stolen T-shirt of the day—showing a rattlesnake with the words *DON'T RATTLE ME*. Circadia and I both inhaled a sharp gasp as we realized what Nighmeria was holding—with its needle antennae and metal abdomen, there was no doubt that Coco's pet Worrywort was holding its own pet Lockcrawler.

Suddenly, from above, we heard music.

"Winks," whispered Circadia. "He's up on the catwalk, and he seems to be humming the theme from one of those spy movies Luna's dads like to watch."

Sure enough, there was Winks, tightrope walking along

the catwalk, doing spins and shimmies. He made his way to a sandbag attached to a rope, took out a large pair of scissors, and began cutting. Just as the rope snapped, he whisper-yelled, "*Le Saboteur!*" The sandbag fell, missing Coco by several feet, and Winks covered himself with his cape like a vampire being exposed to the sun.

"That weirdo conductor guy knows we can see him, right?" Coco asked one of his sidekicks.

"Should we do something about him, boss?"

"Nah," said Coco, "I think he's pretty harmless. And funny. He's my own little court jester. I can't imagine him doing any real damage."

As soon as Coco had said the words, all the doors to the theatre started opening and slamming shut on their own.

"Hey! What was that?" asked Coco.

Suddenly, the stuffing started bursting from the seats in firework-like explosions. The sandbag's rope rose up on its own like a charmed snake and began hissing at Coco, who had gotten up from his throne.

"Here, take this!" said Coco, offering Nighmeria to the rope like a sacrifice.

Finally, when the stage curtains started rising up like ghosts and making "OoooOoooOoo" sounds, Coco threw Nighmeria to the floor and rushed off the stage. His flunkies followed, attempting to fight off the velvet ghouls and hissing ropes.

"How . . . how in the world did Winks do that?" asked Circadia.

"He didn't," I said, lovingly patting the old wood of the stage floor. "I don't think our miraculous Lunarian Grand has lost all of its magic after all."

Chapter Twenty-two

THE LOCKCRAWLER AND THE NOT-A-TRAP TRAPDOOR

Out of the darkness came Nighmeria, chasing frantically after her pet Lockcrawler. As they whizzed by, I stuck out my foot and caught the Lockcrawler by the end of one needle-like leg with the toe of my shoe.

"Nice catch!" said Circadia.

I picked up the Lockcrawler the same way one might lift a cockroach (using the tips of my fingers, a look of disgust on my face), and we made our way over to the trapdoor. As I stared down at it, considering the best way to use the Lockcrawler, Circadia played defense against Nighmeria.

"Oooh, blocked again!" she said, swatting away the Worrywort. "Too slow," she said, diving in front once more like a soccer player at the goal. "Is that all you've got? IS THAT ALL YOU'VE GOT?!"

I took my opportunity and placed the Lockcrawler on the floor. It didn't immediately run away or up my leg as I'd feared it might, but instead beelined straight for a suddenly-not-invisible trapdoor. It did several rapid laps with its metal antennae flying wildly and its legs tapping, seeking without eyes. Finally it found what it seemed to desire more than anything: the keyhole.

"The eagle has landed!" I yelled back to Circadia, whose eyes were now covered by the yowling Worrywort on her head. "The cake is in the oven!"

Once the Lockcrawler had disappeared inside the keyhole, things got very quiet, and I worried that it had merely escaped without doing its job. Circadia managed to trap Nighmeria in a pen of large props, and we both leaned over the door to watch. The lock began to twitch and shudder as if . . . well, as if it had a bug up its pants. There was a series of mechanical shifting sounds, and finally, after a few more moments, the trapdoor slapped open in a fit of disgust.

"Not-a-Trap Trapdoor," said Circadia, reading from a label on the underside of the door.

"I feel like that's exactly what a trapdoor that *was* a trap would say to trick us," I replied as the platform inside the opening started to lower slowly into the floor.

But Circadia wasn't listening. She had hopped onto the moving platform.

"Wait for me," I said nervously, stepping on beside her.

We descended slowly (very slowly) into the darkness, and as we did, elevator Muzak started playing. You know, the kind that's a song you sort of recognize, but it's much slower and without any singing, so you feel like falling asleep. It was *that* music.

"Not that I'm afraid of the dark," I said, "but is this creepy? Descending into nothingness? Does it only bother *me*?"

"Don't worry," said Circadia, "I have a portable lightbulb."

"That sounds very unsafe, very glass, very breakable," I answered into the darkness.

A few minutes later light started to appear at the bottom of the door. "Ooh, I think we're here," said Circadia. She crouched down, trying to see what was below. "It's fine down here, totally normal. Just a street and some houses and stuff."

"It does not sound totally normal," I said, "to have a street and houses beneath a theatre."

But lo and behold, once the platform came to a stop, I saw that there was in fact a street with green grass and various adorable buildings that looked straight out of a nursery rhyme.

"Memory Lane," said Circadia, reading the street sign. "Charming."

As we walked along, I began to notice there was a

theme to all the adorable buildings—and a strange one at that. There was a house covered in stones that looked like peppermints with a shop sign that read *DISCONTINUED HARD CANDIES*, and another with roof shingles made of various floral dinner plates and a sign that read *PLATES WE DO NOT USE*. There was a wee building with every shape imaginable of soap, a shop with endless framed photos of Luna, and finally a building that was covered—every last inch of it—in doilies.

"Do you think someone crocheted all that?" asked Circadia. "It would take an awfully long time. Unless you could speed-crochet like Luna's grandmother."

"Oh. My. Gosh," I gasped. "That's it! This Memory Lane is Lita-themed. Do you smell that?" I asked, sniffing the air. "It smells like pancakes and syrup and . . . butterscotch candies. Exactly how Luna says her Lita's house smells."

Suddenly, *THE HOUSE OF DOILIES* began to shudder, and we discovered Nighmeria clawing away an entire wall up to the window's delicate lace shutters.

"Stop stalking us," said Circadia, lifting the creature. It growled and scratched and coughed up several balls of fabric while we went back up the elevator to deposit the devilish creature onto the stage again.

We then traveled down from the trapdoor once more, again very slowly, listening to more Muzak. But once we arrived, we both looked around, then at each other, then back at the lift.

"Did we. . . . somehow take a wrong turn?" I asked. The sign for Memory Lane was where we left it, but the street had changed entirely. It was still covered in small, adorable buildings, but they were now all magician-themed: *ABRA & CADABRA'S, MR. RABBIT'S TOP HAT REAL ESTATE, WANDS 'N' BEYONDS*, and so on.

"Luna did have that magician phase," I said.

"Maybe we should experiment," said Circadia.

And so we did. We traveled up and down the excruciatingly slow lift, Muzak and all, several more times, and wouldn't you know it, Memory Lane changed each time—to a street of various sandcastles (calming), then carnival-themed tents (fun), then dentist offices shaped like teeth (horrifying), and finally a street of buildings shaped like beehives and honey jars.

"Memories of her beekeeping phase," I said, breathing a sigh of relief. "Let's just stick with this one. I can't go back to those teeth . . . and the drilling sounds . . ."

We read the signs aloud as we walked: *HONEY HUT, FLOWERS 'R' US, WASP PAPER STATIONERY AND NOTE-BOOKS*. The smell of honey filled the air, and we passed several buildings housing exotic plants. We lingered in front of one open-air garden shop called NECTAR NEST, reading the names of the different flowering plants.

"Inkberry," I read, "used as writing ink, very fragrant. Loxphlox grows keys. Forget-Me-Snot nectar reminds you of a loved one"

"Thwackberry," read Circadia. "Whimrose, Glasswort, Weazelsnout, and Centiweed."

We watched the Centiweed walk along a leaf, spindly legs scurrying.

"I think that one's just . . . a regular centipede?" said Circadia.

"Well, no imagination is perfect." I shrugged.

Finally, at the end of the lane, we reached the largest tree I'd ever seen. Giant colorful toadstools grew by the steps that led up to a doorway in the trunk, and they seemed to turn their heads ever so slightly to look at us. More stairs wrapped in and out of the tree, and from every branch hung flowers with endless honeybees collecting nectar and carrying it away. Their constant buzzing created a surprisingly soothing, gentle hum. It was possibly the coziest place I'd ever seen.

The sign over the door read: *THE MEMORY BANK.*

We had arrived at our leafy, bee-and-toadstool-covered destination.

Chapter Twenty-three
BLOOMWIT AND WORMWOOD

A bell over the door chimed as we entered the Memory Bank. Inside, the big, round room contained a warm fireplace, overstuffed armchairs, towers of tea boxes, old pumpkins, mounds of herbs, mountains of newspapers, and great teetering skyscrapers of china cups and plates.

"I don't know why," I said, "but I was expecting it to be more bank-y. You know, tellers, a vault, stacks of coins, free lollipops. This looks like a place where giant pack-rats would live."

"Well, what is a memory, really," asked Circadia, "if not items saved by a packrat brain?"

A spiral staircase led both up and down from the room, and every inch of wall was covered with potion bottles. They were every color, size, shape, and type imaginable, and made a sort of stained-glass effect. And all around the potion bottles zoomed bees—so many that I could never count them. They visited one bottle, then the next, and then zoomed away. There were even landings along the way with doorways leading, I assumed, to even more potions. Some of the bottles looked good enough to eat, and I saw Circadia reach out, her curious fingers brushing a small bottle shaped like a fig.

"I wouldn't do that if I were you-HOO-HOO," said a deep, ominous voice behind us.

We both turned to find a large owl nestled on a perch above the fireplace, seemingly warming its feathers. It wasn't a typical owl, since its feathers were covered with patterns of crescent moons and constellations, and on its head was a poof of feathers with iridescent sparkles on the ends, giving the effect of shooting stars.

"Are you a . . ." I started.

"A Night Owl, yes," said the owl. "Name's Bloomwit, Memory Vault Keeper, Order of Owls, First Class."

"Fancy," said Circadia. "Sounds like you're exactly the individual who can help us. We're looking for a memory."

"Yes, yes," said Bloomwit, taking out a pad of paper and holding a quilled pen in one talon. "Exactly what are you looking for? Give me a clue-HOO-HOO."

"We're looking for a memory of Luna's that contains her dog, Murph," Circadia answered.

"Preferably a happy one," I added.

"Well, let's see what we have, shall we?" The owl then crunched the paper into a tight ball as if she was going to shoot it into the trash, but instead shoved the wad into her beak and ate it. She finished with a loud BURP!

"Let's give that a moment to stew-HOO-HOO," said the owl. With that, she closed her large yellow eyes and started swaying and chanting as if she were at a séance or smooth jazz concert. Then, suddenly, the owl went perfectly still.

"Is she asleep?" whispered Circadia out the side of her mouth.

"I HAVE THE ANSWER, I DO-HOO-HOO!" shouted Bloomwit, her eyes snapping open. She gave a terrible I-have-a-hairball-cough once. Twice. Three times. Then she produced a spit-covered pellet of paper and dropped it into her own open wing.

"Hmmm," said Bloomwit as she unfurled the slimy paper and tried to read the spittle-smudged ink. The owl paused for dramatic effect, which as a theatre-devotee, I admit I appreciated, then whispered, "*Who?*"

The performance was wasted on Circadia, however. "Are you saying 'Hoo' in an owl-type way, or asking 'Who' in a question way?"

"WHO?" repeated Bloomwit, reading the paper. "WHO? WHO?!"

"Could we, um . . . possibly get a second opinion?" I asked.

"Preferably from someone who doesn't keep their filing system in their digestive tract," added Circadia.

"Prognostication Pellets don't make mistakes," scowled Bloomwit. "But if you'd truly like a second opinion, then you may speak to my co-vaultkeeper, an Early Bird named Wormwood. I'll just go get her now."

But instead of leaving, Bloomwit simply burrowed her head under her wing.

"Is she sleeping *again*?" asked Circadia. "This bank has a very lax break policy for employees."

But Bloomwit didn't stay asleep. Her body began to twitch, and her feathers began to flutter, and before our eyes her wings began to change color—from deep blue with moons and stars, to bright orange and red tipped with yellow, each wing now looking like it was a blazing flame-colored sunrise. The plumes on her head smoothed flat, and when she finally pulled her face from beneath her wing, it had changed to that of a cross between a woodpecker and a toucan, its beak hard and strong but colored like a pastel rainbow.

I'll admit it: Circadia and I both screamed, but just a little.

"Wormwood at your service, Memory Vault Keeper, Order of Early Birds," said the bird. Her voice had changed from deep and spooky to high and chipper, and she reached to take a sip from a mug that read *COFFEE: BECAUSE MEMORIES OF MONDAYS HAPPEN.*

"Hi, hello," said Circadia. "Big fan of your whole Night Owl/Early Bird/Jekyll-Hyde vibe. But also, we're kind of on a time crunch, and we're looking for a memory of a dog named Murph. Could you possibly . . . find him for us?"

"Certainly! Faster than fast!" The bird flew up, her magnificent rainbow tail flowing down behind her, and started perching on various shelves around the room. She seemed to be trying to find the right one, and then, to our surprise, she began bashing her beak against a row of potion bottles, one after the other.

"She's going to get a concussion," I said.

"Don't worry!" shouted the bird. "I'm not hurting the memory ingredients!"

But as she said this, one of the bottles twisted, tipped, and plummeted to the ground, smashing with a deafening crash. Into the air floated a mist of words: *BOISE, BALTIMORE, BATON ROUGE . . .*

I sighed. "Great, now Luna has to relearn the *B*-lettered state capitals on top of everything else."

After each beak-knocking session, the bird would put the side of her head to the bottle as if she were listening for something crawling around inside.

"Not here," said the bird, moving to another cabinet.

"Unthinkable," she said, moving again.

"Incomprehensible.

"Unheard of.

"Nope. No. Nada.

"Nothing with Murph here!" Wormwood said, finally returning to her perch and taking another swig of coffee.

"There's got to be a better way to do this," I said, becoming frustrated. "Are spitwads and head bashing truly the best way to find a memory?"

"The best way to find a memory!" squawked Wormwood. "Who knows?! Memories are wild things, almost completely uncontrollable. Sometimes a memory builds a nest in your gutter, or leaves prints in the mud, or sings loudly far too early in the morning. Not a lot of people know this, but a memory, no matter where it is dropped, can find its way home from miles away. You may have heard the stories: A family moves, and a memory is left behind. Then, miraculously, it shows up, months later, nobody knows how. There are the sad stories too; stories of unwanted memories, thrown away. Memories forced to scurry into alleyways to hide. But if, from the corner of that alley, a memory should hear a certain song, smell a certain smell, it rises and sniffs its way back to the source."

"So . . . what does this all mean?" I asked, scared to hear the answer.

"It means," said Wormwood, "that all Luna's memories of Murph the dog are gone. Perhaps they are lost. Or were stolen. Nobody can predict when or if they will return. Perhaps . . ."

From somewhere deep inside of Wormwood came the deep, ominous voice of Bloomwit the Night Owl:

"Perhaps they never do-HOO-HOO."

Chapter Twenty-four
SANDBARS

"**O**kay, but certainly not *all* the memories of Murph,"
I said quickly, alarm overwhelming me. "Even the
one where Murph saw fall for the first time, and ran
around barking at the yellow leaves that were twinkling
down like snow, trying to catch them in his mouth?"

Wormwood flew around, checking various bottles.

"Yes, even that one is gone," said the bird.

"Okay, but what about the one where Murph was a
puppy in puppy class?" asked Circadia. "And all the other
dogs would run around together, but Murph would just
lie all lazy next to Luna, tail wagging, watching the other
dogs play and do tricks like they were a show. That can't
be gone—no way. That was hilarious."

Wormwood checked once again, and again returned
crestfallen.

"Not here, sorry," said the bird.

This continued for some time, with Circadia and me
taking turns asking:

"Even the one where Luna and her dads are watching a movie, and someone on-screen shouted 'GET DOWN!' and Murph instantly got down off the couch and laid flat on the floor?"

"Even the one where Murph snuck to the neighbor's house and stole an entire rack of ribs from beside their grill? And Luna had to bring him over to apologize? And the people weren't even mad, and they couldn't stop laughing because they thought they had hungry ghosts in their house?"

"Even the one where Murph took his first bath? Even the one where Murph saw the ocean for the first time and walked out on the pier, and fell into the water? Even the one when Luna first saw Murph? And he was just a little guy, and he was sleeping in his giant food bowl? And he looked at her with those tortoise-shell brown eyes, and she knew they were SOUL MATES?!"

But after each question Wormwood would check, get a disappointed look on her face, and report back that, indeed, that one was gone too.

"Well, thanks for your help," I said, my voice nearly a whisper. "I guess we'll head back . . ." I wanted to say "home," but I wasn't even sure where that was now, so I just said, ". . . back to the theatre."

Circadia and I made our way back in silence, both, I assumed, mourning such a momentous loss for Luna.

Once the trapdoor elevator had ushered us back to the stage—which was thankfully still empty of Bad

Dreams—we made our way to the screening room to check in with Dozer, who was, to our shock and amazement, awake when we arrived.

"Dozer, you're . . . so . . . conscious," I said.

"I know, it's horrible," he replied, "but I've been watching the Newsreel, and you've got to see this. It's really bad."

The screening room had redecorated itself once again and was wearing its most horrifying ensemble yet. It now looked (and smelled) just like the back basement at Luna's house. Luna's house had a regular basement with a washer and dryer and Ping-Pong table, but there was another basement room behind that with all sorts of water heaters and other machinery. Luna had always been sure it was haunted. She'd never seen an actual ghost or anything, but she just knew from the way it gave her the willies. And now the screening room had cement walls, and a dirt floor, and a water heater, and felt totally ghoul-infested.

We all looked up at the screen, where a scene was playing out between Luna and her dads. They were at the beach, walking away from the shore across a bridge of sand and out onto a large sandbar. They all looked particularly miserable, maybe because of sadness or maybe because it was cold out—we could tell by their warm jackets and red cheeks and the way Luna's hair flew around her head. Under one arm, Luna's dad Ted carried a silver bottle of some sort, shaped like an egg with a flat base.

"It's called an urn," whispered Dozer solemnly, "and inside are Murph's ashes, which Luna has been too scared to look at. They're going to scatter them on the sandbar."

"Whoa," said Circadia. "Heavy stuff."

"But that's not the really bad part," said Dozer, sounding like he might cry. "Just listen."

On the screen, Luna and her dads had reached the far end of the sandbar, and in front of them was open gray-green ocean. The sandbar looked the same as it had looked on all their visits. There were shallow tidal pools and hermit crabs, perfectly polished stones, and the odd piece of glass worn smooth. There were two horseshoe crabs stranded on their backs, which Luna's papa righted and set back into the water. And there was the peace, the perfect quiet except for the sound of the wind and the screech of a seagull every so often, asking what this group of people was doing so far away from the shore.

A sandbar, I thought, is a lot like emotions. It appears seemingly out of nowhere, this small stretch of sand surrounded by water. But then, with the change of the tide, it's gone a few hours later, covered in seawater, as if it had never happened. And that was how Luna's sadness over losing Murph seemed to me—she would almost seem like her normal self for a while, and then there it was, something that reminded her of Murph—maybe a dog on TV, or a stick, or a carrot—and the sadness appeared again. I'd heard that time eased pain. Maybe it would be like that for Luna; maybe time would lap away at the edges of her loss, like waves over a sandbar.

"How does this look?" asked Luna's papa Matías. "You always said how you liked the way you and Murph's footprints would circle around the sandbar like a trail on an old treasure map."

Luna gave her father a quizzical look. "I don't remember saying that."

"We should say something, about Murph," continued Matías. "I brought a poem I could read. 'Long Point Light,' the one about the lighthouse at the end of town, the one you can see from your room at night. You used to read it to Murph on the beach."

"I remember the poem," said Luna, "but not reading it to Murph."

"Is there anything special you'd like to say, sweetie?" asked Ted. "Some words about Murph before we scatter the ashes? Maybe a favorite memory? I think he would like that. He loved you so, so much."

"Um, I suppose I could say something," said Luna. "A favorite memory . . ."

Matías and Ted stood, waiting, watching over Luna as she thought. Seconds passed, then minutes, and finally her dads exchanged worried looks.

"It's okay if it's too hard," said Ted. "Or if you're not ready. We could come back another day."

"It's not that I don't *want* to say a favorite memory

about Murph," said Luna, her eyes filling with tears. "It's that I can't . . . I can't remember any."

"I know it seems that way now," said Matías, "but all those good memories are still there, you just have to give yourself time. Remember saying that Murph's feet smelled like Fritos? Or the way Murph's tail was always dragging in the dew? Or how he'd pretend he didn't dig a hole in the yard, but his nose would be covered in dirt?"

"I want to remember those things," said Luna, "but every time I try to picture them, they're not there. All I can see is nothing. All I can hear is the sound of the truck's tires screeching, the sound of my own voice screaming. I . . . I can't see Murph at all!"

Luna looked down at the sandbar. She tried to picture her footprints beside Murph's in the wet sand, but all she saw were her own. Where had Murph's gone? Had they been taken forever, washed away by the waves of grief? Luna saw that her own prints weren't permanent either; even those were slowly being erased by the water and the waves and would soon be just a memory. *Is there anything*, she wondered, *anything at all that can last for always?*

Chapter Twenty-five

TURNIPHEADED, SLUDGELY, GORMLESS, BIFFLING, MANDRAKE-BRAINED, FLABWINKED FOOL

After we watched the sad Newsreel about the sandbar, Circadia and I decided to go check on the rest of the theatre and spy on the Bad Dreams. We found them onstage, taking a break from what looked like a nightmare rehearsal and making a mockery of our beloved Lunarian Grand.

"We should really change the name of this theatre," Coco was saying. "The Lunarian Grand? It sounds like the name of a ready-to-assemble Swedish lamp."

"Well, um," said one of the other Bad Dreams, "the girl who's dreaming is named Luna, so I think that's why it's Lunarian, and—"

"Zip it, Greeph! Why don't you go write a poem about it!" said Coco, eliciting laughter from all the other Bad Dreams. They all proceeded to throw used food wrappers at this Greeph creature.

Greeph didn't look like the rest of the Bad Dreams— not like Rodenkirk, who looked like a rat; or Tadtroll, who looked like a frog-headed goblin; or Maleficara, who was shrouded in a cloud of darkness; or even Glüm, who was giant, and empty-eyed, and never seemed to say or do anything at all. Greeph looked like, well, a mess. His entire being seemed to be a tangled knot of things. He was a jumbled, mishmashed figure, from the top of his disheveled head to the bottom of his snarled and furry feet. But what struck me most of all was that he seemed hurt by Coco's words and retreated to the corner of the stage, where he released Nighmeria from her cage and pet her as she purred and rubbed her head against his hand.

"That Greeph one doesn't seem quite as bad as the rest," I whispered. "Wonder what his story is . . . wait . . . uh-oh."

Nighmeria had leaped from Greeph's lap and locked her eyes on us, creeping closer, legs tense, belly to the stage. She looked like a lion stalking her prey.

"Go away, get outta here!" I said to the ready-to-pounce Worrywort.

"Hiss! Hiss!" said Circadia.

But this just made Nighmeria more excited, which drew more attention, which led to Coco flinging the curtain aside and finding the two of us cowering there, hissing at a ball of fluff.

"What have we got here?" said Coco, hauling us both up using one of his claws under each of our collars. "Snoops of the Lun-eerie-an Bland? Eavesdroppers of the Boo-narian Grand?"

Circadia and I both crinkled up our noses.

"We're working on the new name!" said Coco, more than a little defensiveness in his voice. "Tell me what you two are doing creeping around or I'll . . . I'll feed you to Bogsby!"

Everyone turned toward the back of the stage where the individual they referred to as Bogsby—who to my eyes looked like a tub full of swamp slime—gave a loud burp of green bubble. It floated into the air, its sulfurous scent coming closer, and when it popped, it said the word *YUM!* as everyone tried not to gag from the smell.

"No, no need for that, we're not yum," I said. "This is my friend Circadia, who is here for moral support, because I, Dormir, am here . . . to . . . audition. To be an actor." *Yes, that's good,* I thought. *A new idea!* "An actor . . . in the Bad Dreams."

In my personal opinion, the solid two minutes of

laughter that followed my proclamation were unwarranted, unhelpful, and most of all, unfair. Sure, I was scrawny, and shy, and a lowlier-than-low assistant, but really? *Two minutes?!*

"Okay, sure," said Coco, wiping the laughter-tears from his eyes. "You can audition. You're clearly very funny. So, go ahead. Show us just how *bad* you can be. Give us your best insults, your evilest affronts, your worst abuse."

The Bad Dreams settled down on various seats and crates around the stage, all eyes on me. Even Nighmeria took a break from licking her bum and grooming herself to pay attention to my impending humiliation.

"Um, insults?" I mumbled. "Sure. I know lots of insults."

I looked to Circadia, who gave me a supportive thumbs-up, and tried to think of literally any insult I'd ever heard. A boy in first grade had once called Luna a bookworm because she was always reading at recess. No! That's hardly an insult, since worms are nature's recyclers, and books are wonderful! I wiped my forehead, sweat wetting my already clammy hands. *You're just going to have to do it,* I told myself, *be daringly rude.* And so, I shouted, so loud it shook the banisters and rattled the roof:

"YOU TURNIPHEADED, SLUDGELY, GORMLESS, BIFFLING, MANDRAKE-BRAINED, FLABWINKED FOOL!!!"

Chapter Twenty-six

A STAR IS TORN

"That was . . . wow," said Coco, his eyes wide. "Never in all my years of being a Bad Dream have I seen something so positively, utterly, absolutely, radiantly . . . *awful*."

Cue a round of record-breaking laughter. They laughed for at least five minutes this time.

"But the truth is," said Coco, "we *are* looking for a new member of the Bad Dreams. An underling of the unkind. A minion of misery. A lowly assistant, if you will, which is a role I've heard you're great at. But you'll have to audition for that as well. Tonight, midnight, the spookiest time. You'll have to show us you're really one of us before we'll let you do our laundry and massage our feet. Understood?"

"Of course," I said, "I understand. Midnight. I'll be there. Thanks for the second chance and OooOooh," I said, twirling my fingers and trying (and failing) to sound like a spooky ghost. Luckily Circadia grabbed my elbow and led me away before I could embarrass myself any further.

"Have. You. Lost. Your. MIND?" she gasped. "You want to join the Bad Dreams?!"

"No," I replied. "I want to *infiltrate* the Bad Dreams. Remember what the Memory Vault Keepers said? All of Luna's memories of Murph the dog are gone—maybe stolen! If anyone would steal Luna's memories it would be Coco, right? If I join them, I'll be on the inside, and can find out the truth."

"Hmm," said Circadia. "It's not a bad plan, actually. I mean, if the Bad Dreams took the memories . . . and they never give them back . . . and Luna is never happy again . . . then they get to stay and take over the Lunarian Grand. You may be onto something."

As we walked back to the screening room, I was lost in thought. *Bad,* I thought. *What did I know about being B-A-D, which is how Luna and her dads used to spell out the word instead of saying it, so Murph didn't think he was being scolded.*

When we arrived, the screening room greeted us with cobwebs. *Lots* of cobwebs. It was like the room had hired a decorator, and that decorator was EVERY SPIDER IN EXISTENCE. Spun silk stretched from the ceiling to the seats, and all around the screen. Circadia and I tried unsuccessfully to crawl through to Dozer without getting caught in the sticky décor. When we found him, he was fast asleep, using a thick spiderweb as a blanket.

"Did we miss anything on-screen?" asked Circadia, trying to shake him but getting her hand covered in web instead. "Dozer, what's going on with Luna?!"

"Oh, you're back," said Dozer with a yawn. "Let's see . . . last reel, she was at her gramma Lita's house for the night and they were making coconut date bars, Luna's favorite, but she looked pretty miserable the whole time. She still can't remember good times with Murph. She saw a spider and trapped it under a glass and released it. How was your walk?"

"It's a long story, and not nearly as delightful as a baking date with Lita," I said, "but the punch line is pretty dramatic—I think I'm auditioning for the Bad Dreams."

"Whoa," said Dozer. "Dramatic is right."

"DID SOMEONE SAY DRAMAAAAATIC?" asked a startling voice from above.

Winks was, somehow, lowering himself from the ceiling vent.

"Winks!" we all shouted as he crashed to the floor. I noticed he'd added to his ensemble since we'd last seen him, now wearing a sparkly bandana around his head, a sword brooch, and what I suspected were shoulder pads under his cape.

"I'm so relieved you're okay," I said. "But you should really use the door."

"*Le Saboteur* makes no promises," said Winks. "But never mind that. What's this I hear about you auditioning for the Bad Dreams?"

116

"It's our plan," I said. "I'll infiltrate the Bad Dreams and see if Coco stole Luna's memories of Murph, which we strongly suspect. Except it's never going to work because I need to pretend to be a baddie. A bully. A threat. And I'm not particularly good at any of those things."

"Well, you know," said Winks, "I've been bullied a fair share in my time. Shocking, I know, but sometimes people just can't handle a personality as vibrant as my own. I can train you."

We all stared at him blankly, having no idea what this meant.

"I'll train you to be the bully!" he explained. "To tyrannize. To torment!"

And, because it was Winks, and I knew that saying no was not an actual option, I agreed to his tutelage even though it immediately felt like a bad idea.

First, he made me change into the outfit he was wearing—sword brooch and shoulder-padded cape and all.

"I look ridiculous," I said, staring into the mirror.

"You look mysterious," said Winks. "Dangerous. Artistic. *Tortured.*"

His first round of training involved me learning to channel my inner nightmare.

"Nightmares," said Winks, "usually fall into a few basic categories: being chased, exams, snakes, teeth falling out . . . humans are very predictable. We'll just train you in those things while we whip you into tip-top physical shape."

And so, he had me jump rope with a snake, practice not losing my teeth, and run at full speed to reach an exam I hadn't studied for.

Next we stood in front of a full-length mirror, fetched from the props department, and Winks told me to insult myself.

"Um," I said, glancing at my reflection, "I suppose I'm quite short. And weak. And nondescript, really."

"Be more descriptive," urged Winks.

"Okay, I'm as boring as an unseasoned side salad and I've got a face like a bag of wet bread."

"Wow," said Winks. "Impressive bullying. Now speak directly *to* yourself."

"You are hot dog water," I said to the me in the mirror. "If Mr. Rogers lived in your neighborhood, he'd probably move. You're as useless as a lighthouse in the desert, as mittens on a fish, as the letter *p* in *pterodactyl*. You're a gray sprinkle on a rainbow cupcake!"

"Now that's what I'm talking about!" said Winks, patting me on the back.

"I feel awful," I said.

"That just means it's working," said Winks. "It means you're ready."

∗　∗　∗

Before we knew it, midnight was upon us.

I made my way to the theatre, and Winks promised

that *Le Saboteur* would be watching and encouraging me from the rafters above the stage. Coco and his co-horts were already there, spray painting their initials on the walls and juggling Fretlettes. The theatre, however, seemed to be on my side; it had adorned itself in a bed of dry leaves, all in reds and oranges and browns, and as I walked, they crunched under my feet in the most satisfying way.

"Thanks, Lunarian," I said, knowing that the theatre was aware of my love of crisp leaves.

"Okay, let's get this over with," said Coco when he saw me. "Kill me with unkindness."

"Right, yeah," I said, shuffling from one foot to the other. "um, so you are Mr. Rogers. No, I'm messing it up, there's hot dog water in the desert . . . No, wait, you're mittens on a pterodactyl . . . a bag of side salad . . . wet sprinkles on a cupcake!"

"NEXT!" shouted Coco. "I mean really, sprinkles on a cupcake? Isn't that basically a disgusting, putrid (gag) COMPLIMENT?"

"No, no, I can do it, I swear," I said. "I did it earlier; Winks helped me."

"Winks!" shouted Coco. "You mean that weirdo who's been lurking in our rafters, spying from the shadows? That complete oddball who actually thinks we can't see him RIGHT THERE?"

Coco pointed up toward the rafter above us, and I saw a flash of black cape as *Le Saboteur* attempted to hide behind a too-thin beam. I wasn't sure what to do, torn between defending Winks and winning over Coco.

As we all stared above, here is what I thought: *How dare Coco say those things about Winks, who is only trying to help Luna? Winks has a huge heart. He's kind, and helpful, and cares about everyone. And talk about talent! What a conductor! He's the life of the party, a snappy dresser, and one of my very best friends. So leave him alone, you putrid, sniveling, lumpy, worm-eaten, slug-slimed, flea ridden jerkface!*

But that's not what I said.

No.

What I said was this:

"I know, right? He's an even bigger weirdo oddball than you'd ever imagine. He cries when his tea is too hot. He's scared of Wednesdays. None of us are really his friends, we just pretend to be to get him to stop talking, which he basically never does. Oh, and the biggest secret of all is that he's only the conductor because he can't morph into a musician or an actor or anything amazing like that. Winks is the least fabulous individual I've ever known."

The Bad Dreams stared at me, wide-eyed. Then, all at once, they burst into wild, roaring, howling, knee-slapping, eye-watering cheers.

"Maybe I underestimated you," said Coco. "That was cruel. That was heartless. That was *mean*. You might just be Bad Dream material after all!"

I didn't look up to see Winks's reaction. I couldn't bear it. But if I had, this is what I would have seen:

One of my very best friends, fighting against the tears in his eyes, whispering, *"Way to go, kid. You really knocked 'em dead."*

Chapter Twenty-seven

GREETINGS, FELLOW JERKFACE

And suddenly, I was once again a lowly assistant in a theatre, busier-than-busy, but this time I was in the business of being bad.

"Oh, hey," said Circadia when she found me backstage. "I was thinking, you should take a break so we can strategize our moves now that you're . . ." She lowered her voice to a whisper. "*On the inside.*"

"A break?!" I shouted. "I haven't had a spare minute all day! I still have to unslime Coco's slugs, organize his nose hair clipping collection, shape his earwax into a likeness of the Bermuda Triangle, harvest the eyeball-growing bush, find the deadest fish, and make a chopped splinter-and-poached-misery salad. I'm swamped!"

"Well, you definitely *smell* like a swamp," said Circadia, holding her nose. "So, there's that, I guess."

I sighed. "I'll come find you when I'm done here. Sorry I snapped at you. I think all the badness is rubbing off on me. It's like a deodorant stain, or burrs, or a broken pen. Totally unpleasant. Sticky. Gets everywhere."

"I get it, buddy," said Circadia, patting me on the back. "Ooh, here comes a Bad Dream. You should try to befriend it."

As Circadia left, I turned to see the Bad Dream named Greeph walking my way. Well, walk was a stretch. This creature was doing more of a slime-that-has-gained-sentience-and-is-being-blown-by-a-strong-breeze into my general direction.

"Greetings, fellow jerkface!" I said, trying to sound like I belonged in the Bad Dreams and mostly failing. "I hope you're having a totally miserable day."

To my surprise, the messy monster actually looked hurt by my words.

"Um, I don't actually think you're a jerk," I continued quickly. "I was just trying to fit in. Tough crowd here."

A look of relief flushed over the creature's face. "I know what you mean, I'm the same way. I'm like a floofy bumblebee in a nest of wasps, all the papery sheets of our hive covered in insults and furious words I don't understand."

"You've got a very interesting way of speaking," I said. "Kind of . . . artistic."

"Oh, I am!" said the Bad Dream. "An artist, I mean.

123

Well, an aspiring poet. You wouldn't want to . . . hear some of my writing, would you?"

All I knew about poetry was what Luna learned in school—similes, rhymes, haikus—and mostly what I'd learned was that people are usually pretty bad at writing poetry. But bad poet or not, I did want to make a friend on the inside, so I plastered a giant smile on my face.

"I'd *love* to hear your poetry," I said.

"Okay," said the creature, taking out a crumpled, sweaty piece of paper and flattening it enough to read. "This one is not titled yet, but I'm thinking of calling it 'Greeph.'"

I am Greeph!
My smile is as rusty as a key left in the rain
I fit no keyhole, and all my doors lead to pain
I am Greeph!
I'm gloomy as the morning after a holiday
I'm back to work, I'm bills to pay
I am Greeph!
I'm not just a bad apple, I'm a bad fruit salad
A medley of mold, a mildewed prune ballad
I am Greeph!
I didn't just wake up on the wrong side of the bed
My slippers are softest sorrow, my pillow filled with dread
I am Greeph!
My days are as dark as bottom-of-your-pocket lint
To see my minuscule hope, you'd have to squint
I am Greeph!

They say a broken mirror gives you seven years bad luck
My luck is so broken, the glass could fill a trailer truck
I am Greeph!
I am Greeph!
I am Greeph!

"I honestly can't tell if that poem was really profound," I said, "or really, um, *not.*"

"You basically just described all poetry," replied Greeph.

"Well, it was definitely . . . a poem, then," I continued. "No doubt about it."

Greeph beamed with pride.

"So, your name is Grief?" I asked. "Isn't that a bit . . . dark?"

"Well, it's spelled *G-R-E-E-P-H,*" he replied. "Though I think it's probably spelled wrong because I'm wrong in just about every way. I don't fit in with the other Bad Dreams. Even that poem isn't really true; I only wrote it because Coco said my writing was, quote, 'disgustingly cheerful.' They want me to be mean, and hard, and cold as a bowl of borscht. But I want to drink the moon and sip the stars. I want to lie in the ocean like a buoy lifted by the salt. I want to have friends to drink tea with. I want to be filled with joy at unexpected moments. I'll always be Greeph—no matter how you spell it—but that doesn't mean I don't also deserve to be *H-A-P-P-Y.*"

"You should come have tea with me and my friends in my fort," I blurted, slapping a hand over my mouth the moment it came out. What was I doing inviting ONE OF THEM to TEA at our SECRET HIDEOUT?!

"I'd . . . I'd be honored," said Greeph, his voice clearly choked up with emotion. "I'll bring the tea biscuits. I'll bake them myself if I can sneak around the other Bad Dreams. I hope that's okay."

"Okay?" I asked. "Better than okay. I can't wait. I'll just jot down the location, and we'll all have tea together, and it will be appalling . . . uh, I mean appealing, and horrendous . . . I mean *stupendous,* and awful . . . awfully wonderful to have you to a very frightful-ly delicious teatime. See you, goon, I mean soon. Okay. Yup. Very smooth, Dormir. Bye, now."

I wiped my sweaty brow as I walked away, nervous about what I'd just done but also sure of one thing: I was seriously not cut out for the role of undercover agent.

Chapter Twenty-eight
TEA & GREEPH

"**C**ircaaaadiaaaaaaa!!" I yelled, running full speed toward the fort. "I did a thiiiiing!"

When I reached her, she had a shovel in her hand and was scooping up Fretlettes and Worryworts and making a pile of them away from the fort.

"Ooh, was it deception?" she asked. "Deceit? A plot? A plan? Evil Bad-Dream-style subterfuge?" Even though I was frantic and totally out of breath, I could still tell she was being sarcastic.

"Actually," I panted, "this is going to shock you, but YES. All those things!"

"Whoa, really?" asked Circadia, narrowing her eyes. "Wait a minute, are you evil now? Are you really Coco in disguise??"

She lunged at me and started trying to find a mask seam at the edge of my face and chin, but was, obviously, unsuccessful.

"Get off," I said, "no, I—okay don't say it's a bad idea

until I finish telling you the whole plan—but I invited one of the Bad Dreams here for tea, and—"

"WHAT WERE YOU THINKING THEY'RE GOING TO COME HERE AND EAT US FOR DINNER PROBABLY NOT EVEN DINNER WE'RE JUST A SMALL SNACK OR COCKTAIL MEATBALL FOR THEM WHAT WERE YOU THINKING?"

"I was thinking," I said, "that we could use the opportunity to get information. You know, make nice, befriend one of them, find out what they know about Luna's memories and who stole them. Also, the one I invited is actually pretty nice. He's an aspiring poet."

"That sounds awful too!" said Circadia, though she did seem to be calming down.

"Just act casual," I said. "Don't spook him." I was rather enjoying our role reversal, since Circadia was usually the calm, brilliant one with all the plans, and I was, well, not.

"You don't want *me* to spook *him*," replied Circadia, pointing across prop storage. And there was Greeph, his eyes narrowed, concentrating on the scrap of paper where I'd drawn him a map to find our fort. He somehow looked even larger and messier than usual, like a mountain of garbage, all tangled together with fur, and eyebrows, and shoelaces. He didn't look scary so much as . . .

"Kind of lost and stray looking, isn't he?" said Circadia. "In a horrifyingly giant sort of way. I'm just not sure how we'll know if we can trust him."

We went outside the fort and waved our arms over our

128

heads in a hello to Greeph. In return he smiled from ear to ear and started lumbering toward us like a happy St. Bernard zombie. Once he reached us, he stopped, looking very serious, and without a word he put the piece of paper where I'd drawn him a map into his mouth, chewed, and eventually swallowed it down with a great gulp.

"That's so no Bad Dreams can find it later," he said, whispering, "*and discover your wondrous and magical secret spot.*"

I gave Circadia a *told you so* look, and we all squeezed inside the sandcastle fort. Luckily, the Lunarian seemed to be on my side and wanted us to befriend Greeph, because suddenly the roof of our sandcastle expanded high into the air, high enough to accommodate the biggest of guests. Inside, one of the seats made of sand had grown, and the teakettle and one of the teacups had become Greeph-sized too.

"This place is like the hum inside a hive," said Greeph, "like being under the covers with a flashlight, like finding a word that fits just right in the middle of a messy crossword. I can't believe I was invited. I feel like a page in a book that someone liked enough to dog-ear at the corner."

The now-oversized teakettle started yelling, the water ready and boiling.

"HAIKUS ARE POEMS," screamed the kettle. "WITH SEVENTEEN SYLLABLES. THEY ARE FROM JAPAN. THE FACT I JUST GAVE IS A HAIKU."

"Wow," I said. "The teakettle must *really* like you, Greeph. It never specializes its facts for anyone."

Greeph took out a battered tin and opened the lid. "I was able to sneak away and make some cookies. They're sour-milk-and-mackerel flavored. They came out much better than the time I made mildew-and-cricket flavored, but slightly worse than my pickle-and-pencil-shaving cake. I even decorated them myself."

We all peered inside the tin and pulled out a cookie. They were the size and shape of a teabag, dipped in frosting. There were even strings with little tags like on a real teabag, only these said *For my new best-teas* in Greeph's extraordinarily messy writing.

"Has a very . . . mackerel-forward flavor," I said, taking a bite. "Very touching, thank you."

"You're welcome," said Greeph, a hint of shyness in his voice. "It's nice to meet people who share my love of tea and poetry. I get so lonely with the Bad Dreams. I mean sure, I have my hobbies—writing, knitting, grooming Nighmeria—but when you pretended to be nasty and sneaked your way into the Bad Dreams, I thought: There's someone I could be myself around, maybe."

I choked, cookie crumbs flying from my mouth. Circadia stared at me, her eyes even bigger than usual.

"You . . . you know about that?" I asked.

"Do the other Bad Dreams know?" asked Circadia.

"Oh no, they're very self-absorbed," said Greeph. "They don't notice much—not a stray eyelash on someone's cheek or the charm of a crooked smile. Not the yellow of a honey-colored lantern light or the sunset inside a seashell."

"Why didn't you tell the Bad Dreams about our plan to infiltrate them?" asked Circadia.

"Because you can't talk butterfly with caterpillar people." Greeph shrugged his mountainous shoulders.

"You really are my newest favorite individual," said Circadia.

"So, why did you need to infiltrate the Bad Dreams anyhow?" asked Greeph. "Maybe I can help."

"Now that you mention it," I said, "we were kinda, sorta, just wondering if you know whether Coco stole Luna's memories about Murph from the Memory Bank . . . and where they are . . . and how we get them back . . ."

"Oh, that's easy," said Greeph. "Coco doesn't have them, but he's thrilled that they're missing. I heard him talking all about it. He threw a small, very distasteful 'Bon Voyage, Memories' party. Attendance was, regrettably, mandatory, and the only hors d'oeuvres were deviled spider eggs."

"Why would he be excited about it?" asked Circadia. "It's *awful*."

"Because," said Greeph, "Coco knows that the longer the memories are missing, the more they'll fade away until eventually they'll be gone . . . *forever*."

Chapter Twenty-nine

THE MUSCLES, THE BRAIN, THE LOOKOUT, AND ME

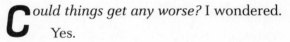

Could *things get any worse?* I wondered.
　　Yes.

The answer was, and apparently always would be: Yes.

We took Greeph to meet Dozer in the screening room, and to see if anything was happening in Luna's life that might give us hope or, as Greeph put it, "make us feel bright as the sun, on top of the world, as pleased as punch."

"The way things have been going," I said, "I'd settle for bright as a dim lightbulb, on top of a slight incline, and as pleased as slightly expired milk."

This time, the screening room was dressed in toadstools that covered every surface. They weren't jolly and red with white dots like the ones in storybooks. No, these were ghost-colored and drooping and tipped in rotting gray fringe.

"Toadstools," said Greeph. "There should be more things named for their use to toads. Toadfork. Toadbook. Toadhat. That last one would be a tiny flower . . ."

Dozer stared wordlessly at Greeph as we introduced them, his usually sleepy eyes wide open. He reached out and shook Greeph's enormous hand, then pulled it back covered in muck and nettles.

"What's the emotional weather like in Luna's world?" Circadia asked Dozer.

"Cloudy with a chance of dogs," said Dozer, wiping his hand on his shirt.

"Well, that sounds fairly positive, right?" I asked.

"You'd think so," replied Dozer, "but no. Luna's world has become flooded with dogs. They're everywhere she turns! It's horrible!"

"But Luna loves dogs," I said.

"Correction," said Dozer, directing our attention to the Daily Newsreel, "she *formerly* loved dogs. Now they're just a painful reminder . . ."

I looked at the screen and felt that old familiar burst of affection. There was Luna, her hair a bit snarly and un-brushed, her face a bit paler than usual, but still her, still my favorite dreamer. She was walking down the side-walk, her tote slung over her shoulder, the straps strain-ing with the weight inside. This meant she'd been to the library, and the librarian had, as usual, let her take out far more than the allowed number of books. *This is good,* I thought. *Maybe Luna is starting to feel like her old self.*

But then, something weird happened. Well, several weird things: First, a woman started walking toward Luna. She was wearing a baby carrier over her chest and was pushing a baby carriage in front of her. But the weird thing—good weird—was that in both the carrier and the carriage there weren't babies but instead French bulldogs. I waited for Luna to completely melt and start dancing around and be absolutely delighted by this. She loved stuff like that! But then the other weird thing happened: Instead of delight, Luna averted her eyes, clutched her tote bag closer, and crossed the street. AWAY FROM THE ADORABLE GRUMPY PUPPIES. It was so unlike Luna, I actually gasped.

"That was . . . odd," said Circadia.

"Oh, that's just the beginning," said Dozer.

We continued to watch as Luna seemed to run into dogs wherever she went—dogs at the park, dogs out car windows, dogs on TV and the covers of magazines. There were dogs on T-shirts, cereal boxes, and in shopping carts at the grocery store. There were even dogs taking form in every other cloud she saw in the sky.

"It's . . . it's . . . an epidemic of dogs!" Luna told her dads.

"Are they mean dogs?" asked her dad Ted.

"Well, no, not that I've seen," said Luna.

"Are they foaming at the mouth?" asked Matías.

"No, no foam," said Luna.

"Are they roaming the streets in packs, stalking prey, howling at the full moon?" asked Ted.

Luna tried to stifle a smile, knowing her dads were being silly. "No, none of that," she said.

"Well then what's the problem?" Matías asked. "You *love* dogs."

"I do . . . I did. It's just that no matter whether it's a tiny Chihuahua or a giant Great Dane, every dog reminds me of Murph and I feel like the world will never be right again."

Luna's dads gave her a big hug, and tried to comfort her, but in the background, I could see a commercial on the TV where a dog was flying with his dog friends, selling who-knows-what.

"I thought dogs couldn't fly in Luna's world," said Greeph.

"Those dogs aren't flying," Circadia explained. "They're just acting. They can make acting dogs fly, drive, dance, play basketball. It's actually very entertaining. Unless of course you're Luna right now, and watching any dog is torture."

"Now that would be great," I said, "if we could just hire that dog from TV to play Murph in Luna's dreams and memories. Maybe then she'd feel better, just seeing him, and remembering all their good times and love."

"I mean . . . could we?" asked Circadia.

"Could we what? Hire a TV dog? Um, no. That's impossible for a zillion reasons," I replied.

"Well, not that specific dog, but aren't there other dogs around in Luna's subconscious?" asked Circadia. "Just hear me out: We find a dog, any dog, somewhere in Luna's subconscious. We train it to play Murph and sneak it into the Memory Bank. Then she'll have Murph memories again and they won't fade away forever."

I stared at Circadia, trying to wrap my head around what she was saying.

"But how would we get it into her memory?" I asked.

"We could do it just like one of those old black-and-white movies Luna's dads are always watching, the ones about bank robberies. You know—there's always an elaborate plan to hit the main vault and steal bars of gold, and it's carried out by a team of experts after months of planning. Except this would be a *reverse* bank heist—we'd be putting a dog *in,* instead of trying to take something out."

"But where would we get a team of experts?" I asked. "We just have . . . um, us."

"*Just* us? You mean, the Muscles," she said, pointing at Greeph, who beamed with pride. "The Brains," she said while motioning to herself. "The Lookout," she said, pointing to Dozer, who was sleeping. "Well, the Lookout-ish," she said. "And . . ."

"And me," I said. "The Nothing."

"Not the Nothing," said Circadia. "You're the One Who

Is Light Enough to Be Lowered Through a Skylight on a Rope."

"Oh, wonderful, what an honor," I said. "Sounds very safe too. But the titles are a moot point anyway, because where do we find this Snory Award–winning dog actor?"

"I HAVE A SNORY-WORTHY IDEA, AS ALWAYS," said a voice from above.

We looked up to see Winks, or as he'd likely be known on our team: the One Who Will Probably Never Forgive Me Because I Was So Very Cruel to Him.

Chapter Thirty
THE QUESTLING BEAST

I barely made eye contact with Winks as he dragged us to the front of the theatre where the marquee loomed above us.

"See," he said, pointing to the sign.

The marquee looked like it hadn't been used in quite some time, cobwebs growing at the edges and only a few random letters left hanging askew or broken.

"I've neglected my duties," said a solemn Dozer.

"In your defense," said Circadia, gently patting Dozer on the back, "the theatre has fallen apart, we haven't had any shows to put on the marquee, and the world is basically ending. I wouldn't be too hard on yourself."

"It said something earlier," Winks told us. "Something about NEWTS."

"Have you been drinking enough water?" asked Circadia. "Getting rest? Spending too much time under the heat of a spotlight?"

"I'm telling you!" said Winks. "It also mentioned BATS."

We all stared up at the marquee as if we were watching a movie but someone had pressed the pause button. Dozer yawned. Circadia adjusted her glasses. I looked sideways at Winks, wishing I knew what to say.

But then, something did happen: A letter *S* crept its way up the marquee like a tiny inchworm, scrunching its back, then flattening, then scrunching again. It finally landed, out of breath, at the top left of the marquee, clearly meaning to be the beginning of a word. Other letters followed the *S,* as if it was the leader of the pack, and soon a few words became clear.

SAY THIS, read the marquee.

Great leaping Lunarians, I thought. *I wished to know what to say to Winks, and now this. Did the marquee read my mind?*

We all watched as the marquee—or more likely, the Lunarian Grand itself—slowly, inchworm letter by inchworm letter, finished what it was trying to tell us.

SAY THIS THREE TIMES:
EYE OF NEWT, SCENT OF HOUND
SOMETHING LOST MUST BE FOUND
SNAKE'S LOW TONGUE, BAT'S HIGH SOUND
QUESTLING BEAST, LOOK AROUND

"Gasp," said Winks. "It has given us . . . a *stage direction.*"

"A spell," said Circadia. "It has *clearly* given us a *spell.*"

"Ah, yes. Also intriguing. What do you think we need?" asked Winks. "A cauldron? Some crows? Maybe a smoke machine for ambiance?"

"I've actually heard that word before," said Circadia, "Questling Beast. It's in the Q volume number seven-hundred-and-forty-two in the dream encyclopedia."

"There's a dream encyclopedia?" I asked.

"Of course. There's a whole encyclopedia wing back-stage," said Circadia, as if this was common knowl-edge.

"*Any*how," she continued, "the book says that Questlings are a thing humans use to remember something when they *kind* of recall it but not really. Like when they say, 'It's on the tip of my tongue,' a Questling is actually look-ing everywhere for it. Apparently, they're masters of disguise, and they change form depending on what the thinker is trying to remember. It could have gills one day and a beak the next. It could hoot or howl, bark or speak in riddles like a parakeet, as it seeks all the things that are just out of memory's reach."

"Thank you, Professor Reads-a-Lot," said Winks. "Now, as far as the spell goes, I volunteer to perform the incantation, as I have perfect articulation." He proceed-ed to do a few vocal warm-ups—some *mee-mee-mee-mee-mees* and some *fa-la-la-la-las*—then got down to business.

"Eye of newt," he said, his voice dramatic and spooky, "scent of hound. Something lost must be found. Snake's low tongue, bat's high sound. Questling Beast, please look around!"

We all huddled together and braced ourselves for the result of the spell. We looked around in every direction, expecting any manner of beast to appear, but slowly it dawned on us that nothing had happened.

"One more time," said Circadia. "Try it louder, Winks! Maybe it didn't hear you."

"EYE OF NEWT, SCENT OF HOUND!" wailed Winks. "SOMETHING LOST MUST BE FOUND. SNAKE'S LOW TONGUE, BAT'S HIGH SOUND. QUESTLING BEAST, PLEASE LOOK AROUND!"

We braced ourselves once again, but once again were met with nothing—no hooves, no paws, no wings beating the air.

"Wait a minute," said Greeph. "Say the last part of the spell again, would you?"

"Questling Beast, please look around," said Winks.

"A-HA!" said Greeph. "I'm a bit of a wordsmith myself, and you're saying it wrong."

"I beg," said Winks, giving Greeph a withering look, "your pardon."

"You're saying 'please,' but that's not in the spell," continued Greeph.

We all looked up at the marquee, and sure enough, there was no *please* to be found.

"Spell or no spell," said Winks, "I'm not going to suddenly become ill-mannered and impolite."

"Greeph's right," said Circadia. "Spells only work if you say them exactly, at least according to every book Luna has ever read and every movie she's ever seen. Let's all do it together."

And so, we all said the spell together, minus the politeness, and stood expectantly once more. But this time, we didn't have to wait long at all.

"Ack!" I yelled as a creature appeared before us, one that wasn't there mere second ago.

It didn't seem twitchy or ready to bolt or any of the other things typical of wild beasts. It was just sitting serenely and tilting its head from side to side as if trying to figure out whether it knew us from somewhere. I noticed it had a bushy ringed tail and pointed snout, but no eyes.

"How is that thing going to find anything," I asked. "It doesn't have any eyes!"

In response, the Questling sprung onto my foot and started voraciously sniffing me with its twitching nose. Without warning, the creature climbed up my leg, stopped to listen to my heart, then settled on my shoulder, investigating my eyes, mouth, and ears. As it sniffed, the creature changed—a kangaroo-pouch formed on its belly holding various-sized butterfly nets, and on its head appeared a hat with *QUESTLING DOG-CATCHING SERVICES* on the front. After braiding a few strands of my hair, tickling my armpits, and knocking on my head as if it was a front door, the Questling jumped back to the ground and sat bolt upright like a dog that had just noticed a squirrel.

"I think we all better get ready to run," said Circadia.

She was right. The Questling seemed to have picked up some sort of scent, and it bolted into the theatre, onto the stage, and toward backstage and all the hallways, twists, and turns.

"To answer your question," panted Circadia as we chased the Questling, "it doesn't need eyes because it sees in a different way. Remember how sometimes Luna's neighbor's cats would hiss at the closet? Or growl at literally nothing and totally freak out Luna?"

"Yes, all the time," I said. "Basically their favorite thing to do."

"Well, they were probably seeing things unseen," said Circadia. "Beasts are very good at seeing the spirit of things. Invisible imprints left by people or ideas. Some creatures can see them clear as day, and the Questling sees them clearest of all."

We all followed the Questling—well, all of us except for Dozer, who stopped for a nap—as it ran through the theatre, hallways, dressing rooms, the costume department, Department of Forgotten Things (which I didn't remember ever seeing, but it looked interesting), and even through prop storage. As we ran, I thought about what Circadia had said about invisible imprints. Perhaps only the Questling Beast could see these imprints, but I was pretty sure the rest of us could *feel* them. There was a dog-shaped imprint in every snowy field Luna passed, in every fluffy pillow, in every pile of leaves.

Maybe there was a Murph-shaped imprint on me as well.

Maybe the Questling had sensed it.

Suddenly, in the set department, the Questling stopped running. We all panted and caught our breath and watched as the Questling pointed its nose and one paw toward something.

"Well, color me shocked," I said.

The Questling Beast had, to my amazement, found us a dog.

Not a well-behaved dog, mind you.

Not a good-looking dog.

Not a dog you'd put on your family's holiday card.

But a dog, nonetheless.

Chapter Thirty-one
THE UNREMEMBERABLES

"**B**ullfrogdog," I said, giving a grim look to the so-called dog in front of us. "I'd forgotten you ever existed. How awful to see you again."

Bullfrogdog simply croaked in reply and kept on happily extending his neck in and out like a balloon. Or a bullfrog. Or a crossover between a dog and a frog, which is what he was, which was as gross as ever.

"Oh yeah!" said Circadia suddenly. "I remember Bullfrogdog! We were all totally scared of him after Luna saw him in a comic book when she was younger. Wasn't he, like, raised in a bog next to a nuclear power plant . . . and was neither wholly frog nor dog . . . It's all coming back to me. What's he doing in the set department?"

"I guess this swamp set must make him feel at home? If he's still lingering in Luna's subconscious, maybe other dogs are too."

We looked around at the set, which must have been constructed by the Bad Dreams for one of their awful shows. It was a gurgling, boiling swamp filled with giant mosquitoes, logs shaped like alligators, trees heavy with Spanish moss, and a general murkiness that was totally unsettling.

"Bullfrogdog could *never* play Murph," I told the Questling Beast, who was now looking at me expectantly. "You'll need to find us something else."

The Questling nodded and took off running once again. We followed it for hours, through the entire theatre, and let me be the first to say that I was shocked—SHOCKED!—to learn how many dogs were lingering in Luna's subconscious. I present to you now . . .

THE UNREMEMBERABLES:
A LIST OF FORGOTTEN DOGS
FOUND IN LUNA'S SUBCONSCIOUS

Bullfrogdog, found being his usual awful self in a bog in the set department

Toto (ironically played by a Great Dane), from Luna's school play of *The Wizard of Oz*, found making its own "yellow brick road" in a back hallway

All the puppies from the *Beethoven* sequels (movie dogs, not composer), found shaking mud all over the playbill wall

A dog from a sad ASPCA commercial, crying into a mirror in Reverie's dressing room, surrounded by lit candles, with very sad music playing in the background

The dog a girl smuggled into summer camp when Luna was seven, found eating fireflies in the lighting department.

Smoochpooch, the stuffed dog Luna had until she was four, when it was deemed EXTREMELY UNSANITARY because Luna had insisted that everyone she met must kiss it, found licking seats in the theatre

Luna's dog-shaped piggy bank made of porcelain, found digging holes in the prop department, burying coins, digging them up again, then re-burying all of them

All twelve dogs from the several-years-expired wall calendar in the bottom of Luna's desk, found in the weather closet sniffing bottles of sunshine, falling leaves, and spring showers

The scary dog down the street who barked at everything, found barking at an abandoned hi-hat cymbal in the orchestra pit, making it clash with nervous shakes

The slightly less scary dog down the street who never barked (eerily quiet), staring at a blank wall in the dark

Luna's former imaginary friend Chewgum's long-lost imaginary dog friend named Shoegum, not exactly found but we did see his collar walking along a corridor as if on an invisible pooch . . .

And finally, the Questling tracked down a Polaroid of Murph, one that had been lost years ago and forgotten, found under a seat cushion in the screening room. As soon as we laid eyes on it, it began to fade away, more and more. *Stay!* I wanted to shout at it. *Sit. Sit. STAY.*

But, just like all the other Unrememberables, it did not.

Like every other dog we found, Murph the photo seemed to exist for just a brief moment while the Questling was looking at it, but once the beast turned its attention away, each dog faded back into the oblivion from which it came.

"The only one I don't think any of us will miss," I said, "is Bullfrogdog."

Chapter Thirty-two

NEW WORTEHAMFORDSHIRE

"**A**re you just going to lie there forever?"

Sigh. It was Circadia. She was standing over me in the screening room, eating pessimism-flavored popcorn, a bewildered look on her face.

"Here, you should eat something." She threw a few pieces of the popcorn at my despondent head. One hit me in the eye. I did not blink.

"Creepy," said Greeph. "Say, Dormir, do you want to hear a poem? Would that cheer you up? I have a new one called 'Everything Is Awful and Will Always Be That Way and You Can't Convince Me Otherwise.'"

Greeph screwed up his face in confusion, looking from his poem to his own bag of popcorn. "I really need to stop eating this stuff," he said, shoveling another clawful into his mouth.

"I'm just going to lie here," I said, "until the moss over-takes me and I am no more."

"I think that floor is actually linoleum," said Circadia.

"I CAN WAIT," I replied.

And that's pretty much how it was. Me, lying on the floor for several days in a row, my friends dining on pessimism and unable to rouse me out of my despair. *This is it*, I thought. T*his is the end of the road. We've tried everything: the Memory Bank, infiltrating the Bad Dreams, finding every dog Luna has ever forgotten . . . and to no avail. We're out of ideas. We're out of hope. And so, I will just lie here like a useless weed while all memories of Murph droop, decay, decompose, and finally disappear forever.*

On the Daily Newsreel, things weren't much better.

"Luna," said her dad Matías on the screen, "you've become a bit . . . how do I put this gently?"

"Creepy," said her dad Ted. "You've been acting super creepy."

"You mean the hoarding all my belongings on my bed with me at night?" asked Luna.

"Well, yes," said her dad. "And also . . ."

"The notebook I've started keeping of all the people I know and where they are at all times?" asked Luna.

"Yeah, definitely," said Ted. But also . . ."

"What?" asked Luna.

"We understand you're still grieving," said Matías, "and we understand, and want you to take all the time you need, but—"

"But," interrupted Ted, "we've notice that you've been watching us sleep. Sometimes I wake up and see you standing there silently across the room like a haunted Victorian ghost. Why don't you just wake one of us up? Are you still having nightmares?"

"Sometimes," said Luna. "But mostly I'm just making sure."

"Making sure?" asked her dads. "Of what?"

"That you're still here!" cried Luna. "That you're okay, and haven't disappeared or . . . or worse, like Murph did. I mean, one day he was here, completely, and the next he was just gone? Forever? I didn't know that that could just happen at any time, and now it's all I think about."

Luna's dads exchanged a look, then gathered her up in their arms, cooing, *We're right here, we're right here,* over and over.

I, too, was remaining right where I was.

On the floor, that is.

After an unidentified number of days, however, I developed what can only be diagnosed as "the will to get up." I'm not sure if it was watching Luna, or the spiders that had started to build webs between the folds of my overalls, but I decided it might be best if I went for a walk. Just a stroll. A very short meander, and then right back to my career of lying on the floor and softly weeping.

I went to the lobby for a few minutes, walked under the marquee, through the theatre, and into the backstage area. I wandered in and out of props and costumes until

I found myself in an unfamiliar corner of set storage that I'd never explored.

"What in the world . . . ?" I mumbled, staring down at the sign at my feet. It was no higher than the top of my boots, and read

WELCOME TO NEW WORTEHAMFORDSHIRE

It seemed that the Worryworts, Fretlettes, and Anxiefleas had built what could only be described as a small, British-looking village of their own. There were shopfronts with forks and spoons serving as columns, several milk carton houses with playing card roofs, anchovy tin swimming pools, thread spool outdoor café tables, and more than a few pumpkins with windows and chimney smoke coming out their stems.

"Hey, watch it, I'm walking here," said a tiny squeak of a voice from below.

I looked down to find that a surly Fretlette was leading a pack of snails around my shoe like a shepherd with his flock of sheep. Apparently, the theatre pests could talk now? They seemed to be getting stronger, which was not good.

I got down on my knees to peer in the shop windows: There was a small bookstore with wee books, a shop selling tiny plants, one with various acorn tops and seashells as dishware, and a pet store selling flies, slugs, moths, ants, and ladybugs. It all reminded me of the tiny towns

Luna would build for her toys when she was younger, the whole place populated by little bear or mouse dolls in dresses and ties. But this was different. This was REAL. This was a group of worries and anxieties and frets taking up permanent residence and setting down roots!

"Get out of here, you disgusting beasts!" yelled a small voice below me. "Shoo!"

I looked down to see a Fretlette wearing an apron and shooing away some smaller creatures with a wee broom. The creatures looked like little winged glow-mice and were gathered around singing songs like carolers.

"Little Rays of Hope," said the Fretlette, looking up at me and rolling its eyes. "They're disgusting creatures, trying to take over the town, always so cheerful. Anyhow, sorry about that. Are you here for the lunch special? Welcome to the Mole Hole."

The Fretlette held out a small piece of paper in my direction. I looked around me and realized I was crouched next to a group of tables and chairs crafted from bent forks, and through the window I could see a café with tables and a counter covered in tiny pastries and cakes.

"Um, thanks," I said, taking the menu, unsure what else to do.

I looked it over: cockroach tripe, acorn tureen of soup, filet of minnow, kernel of corn with lime, balsamic pomegranate seed, six chocolate-coated sprinkles, fried cherry tomato.

"Just a cup of tea, I guess?" I said.

A moment later, the Fretlette brought out half of a quail's eggshell filled with warm mint tea, which I attempted to drink, feeling the slightest hint of mint on my tongue. The waiter had also left a bill, which I attempted to read.

"I'm sorry, does this say, 'a Bother and a Half,' as the amount I owe?" I asked. "Is that like a coin or type of money in, um, New Wortehamfordshire?"

"Yes," said the waiter. "A Bother is the smallest denomination, five of those equals a Concern, two Concerns makes an Annoyance, ten of those gets you a Torment, and it goes on from there, if you're fairly well-off: Terrors, Revulsions, Phobias, and so on. Do you have the payment or not?"

"Maybe . . . yes . . . no . . . I have no idea what we're talking about, actually," I said.

"Just tell me two things that concern you," said the exasperated waiter, "and I can make change."

"Like . . . global warming?" I asked.

"Sure," said the waiter. "And?"

"I guess I'm half-concerned about, um . . . killer bees?"

"Wonderful, exact change," said the waiter, beginning to clear my cup. "Have a fretful day."

I stood up, stretched my back, and moved on down the village road, trying not to step on anyone or anything. A small crescent-moon shaped sign caught my interest. Written on it was the word *LUNARTIFACTS*. I got on my hands and knees again and peered inside the shop, which was more of an open-air market with rows and rows of items. Many, I noticed, looked particularly familiar.

"Hey!" I said. "That's my seashell from my fort! And my marble, my never-dying flower, my wishing penny, my half-used crayon, and my button! Thieves!"

I reached in and started grabbing all the items that belonged to me, shoving them in my pockets. My eyes finally landed on something I was POSITIVE didn't belong here, but rather back in my sandcastle fort: It was the Essence of Murph I'd saved from the Bottle of Scents Room. I picked it up, turning it over in my hands like a tiny treasure, reading the small label with the letters *M-U-R-P-H* like they held some sort of secret.

"I hope you're planning on paying for that, buddy," said the Worrywort behind the counter who was holding a rose stem with a few thorns at its end as, I can only assume, a weapon. "Or are we going to have a problem?"

"Ugh, fine," I said. "How much? My life savings of distress? A vault full of headaches?"

"More than you can afford," said the shopkeeper.

"Try me," I said. "I've been lying on a floor for *days*. I'm rich in unpleasant emotions."

"The cost," said the Fretlette, "is your deepest, darkest fear."

I gulped. Oh good, just what I'd been trying to avoid thinking about while at the same time thinking about constantly. I guess it's like they say: Everywhere you go, there you are. I'd add: There you are, trying to hide from your feelings.

"Easy," I said, taking a deep breath. "My deepest fear is that I'll never mean anything to anyone. That I'll always be a lowlier-than-low nobody and my entire existence will add up to a whole lot of nothing. That I will never help anyone, never realize any potential I might have, and end up cold in the shadows, as far from the warm glow of the spotlight as possible."

The shopkeeper handed me the Essence of Murph bottle.

I guess I had earned it.

Sigh.

Chapter Thirty-three

BEDBOOGS & BROOMSTICKS

I'd barely made my way back from New Wortehamford-shire, when I was grabbed by one of the Bad Dreams and dragged back toward the Director's office.

"Haunted," was all he'd said, as if that was some sort of explanation.

"TH-TH-THERE YOU ARE," thundered Coco when he saw me. He was sitting at a desk, wrapped in layers of fur blankets, his sharp teeth chattering loudly.

"I h-h-hired you as a lowly assistant, a handyperson, a massager of foot fungus, and a fixer of things. And you keep disappearing when I need something fixed. This place is freezing, and every time we try to make a fire, it just . . ."

As way of example, Glüm struck a long match and held it to the newspaper and logs in the fire. The edge of the paper caught, and just when I thought the wood would catch, there was a sound like a giant inhaling, then a WHOOSH! of air, and the fledgling fire was blown out.

"See! It's defective! Devious! D-d-deranged!" said Coco.

"Hmm," I said, looking around for the source of the wind. I noticed that the Director's office had similar curtains to the ones onstage, with beaded eyes open to signal that Luna was awake. Except when I looked at the curtain, one of the eyes, well . . . it *winked* at me. I looked around to see if the Bad Dreams had seen it, but they were too busy arguing amongst themselves.

"Um, the Lunarian Grand can be a bit . . . tricky," I said. "I can try to start the fire if you'd like."

"Oh, you mean D-D-DO YOUR J-J-JOB?" chattered Coco.

I leaned over the fireplace, placing my hand gently on the stone hearth. *It's okay,* I tried to tell the theatre with my touch, *it's just me, old friend.* It must have worked, because when I touched match to paper, there was no great inhale or exhale, and the fire ignited without much bother at all. The Bad Dreams all gathered around, rubbing their hands and facing their tushies toward the warmth.

"Not completely useless, I suppose," grumbled Coco, who had removed a layer of blankets and was beginning to thaw out. "That's not the only thing broken in this malfunctioning theatre," added Coco. "At first it was just a few small things—the howling wind in a windowless room, that owl wallpaper in the hallway screeching at me every time I passed, the dust bunnies that nibble at my toes. I just assumed the place was haunted. How fun! I thought. But no. No! It's . . . it's . . . impolite, this theatre. Inhospitable. Bent on revenge. And not in the way I normally like those things, because now, it's directed at *me*. And *you* need to fix it!"

"Okay . . ." I said, "why don't you show me what else is going on."

"Take my desk here, for example," said Coco.

"Well, the *Director's* desk," I replied.

"My desk has clawed feet, see?" continued Coco, ignoring my clarification. "And sometimes it will start to scratch the floor with those feet or itch its own underside."

As if on cue, the desk lifted and bent one wooden leg and scratched itself.

"Doesn't seem so bad," I said.

"But then other times . . ." said Coco. As he said this, the desk stretched its clawed feet, tilted the front ones forward, and lay down altogether, everything on the desk falling and crashing, coffee spilling everywhere.

"That doesn't seem *so* bad," I said as the sound of light snoring came from the desk. "Probably just needed a nap."

"Ah," said Coco, looking a bit unhinged, "but there's also infinite other tiny things that are driving me OVER THE EDGE. It's death by a million paper cuts with this place! For instance, sometimes when I go to the break room for a coffee, it's just snowing inside. Nothing heavy enough to accumulate or get a snow day, just a light dusting. And there are the doors that used to pull to open that are now push instead. And drawers keep getting stuck, but Glüm puts some muscle into it trying to open one, suddenly the drawer will let go like it was never stuck at all and shoot him across the room. And the carpets sometimes sprout porcupine-like quills. Oh! And whenever I take a book off the shelf and open it, it smells like whatever repulsive thing is going on in the story: a fresh summer's day, or carnival treats, or kittens frolicking in fields of wildflowers! And it lingers for days!"

"I didn't know you could read, boss," said Glüm.

"And it has been cloudy with an occasional drizzle in this office since we moved in," continued Coco, ignoring him.

Again on cue, there was the sound of rumbling thunder in the distance, and a misty rain began spitting on us.

"Yeah," I said, "that all sounds like normal Lunarian Grand stuff. Nothing to be alarmed about."

"I don't get *alarmed*," said Coco. "I'm just . . . *annoyed*."

"And your feelings got hurt, remember, boss?" said Glüm.

Coco glared at Glüm. "Well, the floors here are quite cruel."

"Cruel floors?" I asked.

"Yes, listen!" said Coco, stepping gingerly on the floorboards. When he put his weight down, instead of just creaking, the floors seemed to be creaking *insults*: "*YOOOUUU MEATBALL-MINDED, BEIGE-BRAAAAINED,*

PICKLED SLUUUUUG OF A COCOOOOON-HEADED INTRUUUUDER."

"They're not just creaky," I said, "they're also a bit cheeky." I chuckled. "Ba-doom-CHA."

"BUT WHAT ABOUT THE CHIRPING GHOSTS!" shouted Coco, his hair standing on end. "Listen, can you hear them? They're everywhere. They're in the walls."

The other Bad Dreams went silent, straining to hear whatever Coco was talking about. But I knew better. I grabbed some tissues off the desk and jammed them in my ears.

"I hear it," said Glüm. "A chirp, like a cricket or grass-hopper."

"Oh, I know what that is." I smiled. "It's not a ghost. You're just infested with—"

But before I could finish, Glüm started tapping his feet and moving his hips from side to side. Coco began dancing too—first a light tap dance, which turned into a foxtrot, and ended with Coco grabbing a broom from the corner and using it like a dance partner.

"The office is infested with Bedboogs," I explained. "Their chirping causes the dancing. When Luna was little and too energized to go to bed, her dads would say they were all infested with Bedboogs, and they'd put on music and dance until Luna was tired."

"How did they *stop* the dancing?!" snarled Coco.

"They all pretended to take a potion," I said.

"And do any of you have such a potion?" asked Coco.

"No," I said. "But I know a bird who might. Well, *birds,* really . . ."

"So go get it!" yelled Coco. "I'll give you anything to make this dancing stop. I'll . . . I'll . . . I'll give Luna a night with no nightmares!"

"Whoa," I said. "You've got yourself a deal."

Chapter Thirty-four
ESSENCE OF MURPH

Circadia and I stared forward, slowly descending down the trapdoor and listening to the Muzak.

"Thanks for coming along," I said.

"No problem," said Circadia. "I'd do anything to give Luna a night with no nightmares."

The area outside the Memory Bank had, once again, changed—this time it all seemed themed to Luna's preschool memories. There was a shop selling only PB&J sandwiches with the crusts cut off, a pond filled with swimming fish crackers, a row of buildings made entirely from colorful blocks, and a magnificent road paved with padded mats in dark blue and red.

"Nap mats!" said Circadia. "I loooooved nap time. Should we just have a quick one?"

I gave her an impatient look, and she got up from where she had started to lie down on the ground.

The Memory Bank was now shaped like an oversized backyard playhouse, the walls a bright yellow, the smiling flowers in the window boxes made of hard plastic. The inside, however, was still the same and full of potion bottles, and we found Wormwood bashing her head against a cabinet, attempting to close a drawer.

"Oh no," I whispered to Circadia. "It's the hard-headed clumsy one who breaks memories. That's the *last* thing we need."

Wormwood bashed her beak one last time, then started to fly down from the cavernous expanse of potions, occasionally losing her balance and smashing into a wall, causing several bottles (and I assumed valuable memory ingredients) to collapse.

"I'm starting to understand why Luna can never remember her times tables," I whispered to Circadia.

"We have a question about a make-believe potion," said Circadia when Wormwood reached us.

"Make-believe potion," said Wormwood. "That's another department."

Wormwood burrowed her head beneath her wing, but this time we weren't fooled into thinking she was merely sleeping. Her body began to twitch, and each feather began to change color before our eyes—from bright orange and red tipped to deep blue with moons and stars. Her head sprouted plumes and when she finally pulled her face from beneath her wing, her beak had grown smaller, into the serious face of Bloomwit the Night Owl.

"What can I help you-HOO-HOO with?" asked Bloomwit.

"It's actually a fairly unusual request," I replied. "Luna and her dads used to play a game that involved Bedboogs, and dancing, and a potion. And we were wondering if maybe you could . . . make us the potion?"

While I spoke, Bloomwit had a pen clutched in her clawed foot and was writing furiously. When finished, she took the piece of paper and shoved it into her beak. We all waited until, finally, Bloomwit gave a terrible I-have-a-hairball cough and produced a spit-covered wad of paper into her open wing.

She unfurled the paper and began to read, then fluttered around pulling potion bottles from every corner of the room.

"Elixir of Incoordination," muttered Bloomwit, "Extract of Two Left Feet, and a Perfume of Broken Records."

When all the ingredients were mixed in a vial, the potion let out a small puff of smoke and the sound of drums crashing, then silence. Seemingly pleased with this outcome, Bloomwit put a cork in the bottle and handed it to me.

"Thanks" I said, "this means a lot to us. And to Luna."

"Happy to help," said Bloomwit. "Now if you'll excuse me, I need a nap. I've been having terrible headaches for some reason."

"Actually, there was one more thing," I said, taking out the Essence of Murph bottle I'd bought back in Wortehamfordshire. "I was wondering if you could tell me about this essence. What is it made of? What does it do?"

Bloomwit took the Essence of Murph into her wing, picked up a magnifying glass with the other, and started to study the bottle from every angle. She sniffed it with her beak, licked it with her tongue, and rubbed it against her feathers.

"I've used my extensive psychic background," said Bloomwit, "to find your answer. The Essence of Murph is made up of many things."

Bloomwit proceeded to cough up yet another owl pellet and unfurled it for us to read. It listed things like loyalty, and kindness, and a taste for socks.

"I appreciate this list," I said, "and this all seems very Murph indeed. But . . . um . . . what does it *do?*"

"This essence is made with Nostalgia," explained the owl. "Nostalgia can do lots of things: help with remembering, bring back the past, assist in transformation."

"Hmmm," I said. "What . . . kind of transformation?"

"Well, theoretically," said Bloomwit, "an essence can turn something into the essence's form. For example . . . an Essence of Summer could—again this is theory, no one has ever dared try it—turn someone into a kind of summer. An Essence of Night into night. And, I suppose, this Essence of Murph into a sort of Murph."

Circadia and I exchanged a look of excitement.

"Like one of us could use it to turn into Murph, and play him in one of Luna's dreams or memories . . ." I asked.

"Before you get any big ideas," said Bloomwit, "I

must give you a dire warning: If you use a potion with Nostalgia to change form, you stay in that form . . . permanently."

"But it *could* be done?" I pushed.

"I suppose," said the owl, "but I wouldn't recommend it."

"What exactly *is* Nostalgia?" asked Circadia. "Seems pretty powerful."

"Nostalgia . . ." said Bloomwit thoughtfully, "is not so easy to define. I suppose I'd describe it as something that you loved, but didn't notice how much you loved, at least not at the time it was happening. Maybe you didn't notice because it was so commonplace, regular, or small. Like eating cereal at the table in the morning with your family. Or jumping in piles of leaves in the fall. Or the flavor of the blue Popsicle from the ice-cream truck. It was just cereal and a leaf pile and a Popsicle at the time. But then, one day, you realized it was gone—you and your family hadn't sat down to eat cereal in years, and you never jumped in leaves, and the ice-cream truck stopped coming to your street. And you *miss* it. I mean, not necessarily the specific Popsicle, but rather the feeling of excitement when you heard the truck's music, and how you dashed to grab a few quarters, and the way you ran outside barefoot through the grass and sprinkler to get there in time. You miss a *moment*. A person you were. An age. You miss the smell of Play-Doh or those fruity markers in school. You miss the feeling of water up your nose in the kiddie pool and drawing with sidewalk chalk and just . . . a million little things that equaled a certain time in your life. And one whiff or tiny reminder can bring the entire thing rushing back to you-HOO-HOO."

I knew exactly what Bloomwit meant. I'd just never known the word for that feeling.

"So that's Nostalgia," I said.

"That's Nostalgia," said the owl. "And it's one of the most potent ingredients in the world."

Chapter Thirty-five

A MEMOIR OF MISSING YOU

When we returned to the Director's office, we found the Bad Dreams all still dancing and covered in sweat.

"A deal's a deal," said Coco, clearly sensing that I was considering just letting them dance forever.

"He has an annoying point," said Circadia.

And so, I took out the anti-Bedboog potion, and tried not to gag as I held the bottle for each dancing Bad Dream to drink from. Finally, their dancing began to slow, then stopped altogether.

"It's a miracle," said Coco, collapsing in a heap onto the floor. "You," he said, pointing at me, "aren't as useless as you look."

"Um, thanks."

Coco crawled to the desk as he began to recover, heaving himself into the chair and panting.

"Glüm," he shouted, "massage my feet!"

Glüm did as he was told, even though he was clearly exhausted as well, and Coco motioned for me to sit in one of the chairs opposite the desk. This was usually where the Director made us sit when she was going to yell at one of us, so it was with some deserved worry I took the seat.

"I think . . ." said Coco, stroking his chin, "yes, I think I'm going to give you a promotion. Now, where are we in need of help . . . ?"

While Coco pondered, I wondered: *What exactly did a Bad Dreams promotion entail? Would I be promoted to Badder Dream? Baddest? Are those even words? Would I eventually climb the corporate Nightmare ladder and become the Worst Dream of All?* These were not my kind of career aspirations. I wanted nothing to do with any of that; I wanted out of the Bad Dreams. That is, until Coco said something that nearly knocked me over with surprise.

"An actor!" shouted Coco. "We're in need of an actor. None of my usual team can ever learn their lines. That's why it's all a lot of zombie moaning and beast howling in nightmares: less memorization."

"An actor? Me?!" I choked out. "Are you serious?"

"No, I'm making a hilariously bad and confusing joke," said Coco. "Yes, of course I'm serious! You can start tonight." Coco waved his claws nonchalantly. "Ah, I remember my first time on the stage . . . the putrid smell of the theatre, the tingling excitement as the houselights dimmed . . . standing in that spine-chilling spotlight, feeling like a star, basking in that warm, dazzling, ghastly glow . . ."

✳   ✳   ✳

Glow.

That was the word Coco had used to describe the feeling of being onstage. *Glow.* I'd always imagined what it would feel like to stand in that circle of light, letting it fill me up inside like a warm embrace.

I mean, Coco also used the words putrid, spine-chilling, and ghastly, I thought.

YES, BUT THE GLOW, I thought back at myself.

Perhaps I needed a rest.

I found my way to my sandcastle fort and made myself a warm cup of chamomile and honey tea. "AS THE SUN SETS, IT LOSES ITS BLUE HUES AND BEGINS TO CHANGE INTO GREEN AND YELLOW, THEN ORANGE AND RED. THAT IS HOW A SUNSET GETS ITS GLOW," screamed the kettle when the water was ready. How fitting.

Maybe it would help me relax if I did some light reading, so I browsed through my sand-shaped shelves and found the perfect work—a collection of letters by my favorite author. Ever since she was very young, Luna had written notes and letters to Murph. She wrote them at the end of summer when she left for school, when she went to sleepovers without him, and when she was away at camp. I'd kept copies over the years, reading them from time to time like a beautiful, beloved novel entitled *A Memoir of Missing You*.

Luna's Letters:

Dear Murph,

I am going to a sleepover down the street, and I won't be home all night so I've kissed the page below here three times for you. There's one for bedtime, one for the morning, and one extra just in case.

I love you!

Love,

Luna

Dear Murph,

I am very sorry I yelled at you for eating a butterfly. It just seemed wrong. But I know you don't know what a butterfly is and I forgive you.

I love you,

Luna

P.S. For future reference, they are not food.

Dear Murph,

Well, I'm at sleepaway camp for a whole week. I told you I'd write you every day, so here is your first letter. Maybe you learned to read while I was gone, but if not, have someone read it to you. Camp is different than I thought it would be. My bunkmate is not so nice, and when we talked on the phone in the spring I told her I'm afraid of the top bunk, but when I got there, she and the other girls had taken all the bottom beds and were giggling as I climbed up. Don't worry, I'll be fine. If I fall and break my arms, I'll pet you with my feet.

I miss you.

Love,

Luna

Dear Murph,

Happy Barkday!

Did you know your name isn't really Murph? Well, when we adopted you from the pound, we named you Morpheus, the god of dreams and sleep. But once we got to know you, it seemed too serious for such an unserious kind of guy. So we tried shortening it to Morph, but that sounded like you were a superhero, so finally we landed on Murph, which we decided is short for Murpheus, the lesser-known god of dognaps on your back while lightly kicking your paws and drooling.

You didn't seem to notice the name change. Or if you did, you were very polite about it and went along with us.

Here's to another year together.

Love,

Luna

Dear Murph,

I forgive you for eating my science project.

I understand now that a real erupting volcano made of Rice Krispies Treats was too much of a temptation for you to resist.

Your best friend,

Luna

Dear Murph,

I found the enclosed long white whisker on the floor. Is it yours?

Love,

Luna

The final letter was not a letter at all, but a sealed envelope with the note still locked inside. Luna had kept it secret when she'd written it. She'd licked the envelope and written on the outside:

I stared at the envelope and turned it over and over in my hands. *What was inside?* I'd never know since Murph would never get another Barkday.

But I realized I did already know. Not the letters, or the words, or the lovely and funny thoughts they'd form. But I knew there would be that glow—the glow I longed for, the one I was starting to realize I'd never find with the Bad Dreams, even if they let me become the actor I'd always wanted to be. I was only going to find that glow in places like the folds of this letter, because that glow was in Luna, and it would only shine if Luna smiled again, if her eyes twinkled, if she rediscovered her joy. Hearing her laugh would be like rain on parched, cracked earth, and in that moment I wanted it more than anything— more than knowing what was in the letter, more than standing in any spotlight, even more than being a star.

Chapter Thirty-six

PLANET-SHAPED LOLLIPOPS WITH SUGAR-COATED MOONS

I stood in front of the other Dreamatics trying to summon some confidence.

"I have gathered you all here at the concession stand for an announcement of epic importance."

There was muttering amongst my gathered co-Dreamatics—or at least those I could find—which included Circadia, Dozer, and Winks, as well as non-Dreamatic, Greeph.

"The dictionary defines *concessions* as refreshments that are sold, often during a movie or show," I began, giving the speech I'd rehearsed a dozen times. "And yet, there is a second definition of *concession*: a thing that is granted, especially in response to demands. Now—"

"BOOOOO!" came a voice from my small audience.

"This speech is boring! Bring on the candy!" said someone else.

"AND THE SECOND DEFINITION," I continued, ignoring my friends, "is fitting for our current situation. For our situation demands a hero. And I will grant that concession."

"I fell asleep while I was already sleeping," said Dozer. "That's how bad this speech is."

"Ugh, fine," I said. "Eat some candy, give yourselves a sugar high, and then I'll finish my very interesting speech that I worked on all night."

"Yay!" they all shouted.

But as my fellow Dreamatics began rooting around the concession stand, all I heard were cries of "Gross!" "Ew!" and "Is this even edible?!"

I went over to investigate, and sure enough, everything was in complete disarray.

"Where are all the caramel fireflies with their little blinking butts that made your mouth glow from the inside?" asked Circadia.

"Yeah," said Dozer. "And where are the trixie stix that were basically just flavored sugar that made you have great ideas for April Fools tricks? Those were my favorite."

"THE PLANETS HAVE DISAPPEARED!" said Winks dramatically.

He was right; in the section of the glass concession stand case where there were always planet-shaped lollipops with sugar-coated moons orbiting around them, there were now none to be found.

But there were treats, just not any that I recognized. I started pulling some out, reading their wrappers.

"Feeling of Falling Gummy Fears. Swedish Smells-Like-Fish Candies. Phlegm and Phlegms. Almond Joylessness. Mustache-Flavored Malt Balls. Mustache-*Growing* Malt Balls. Farties. Naked Nougats. Peppermint Ratties. Pre-Licked Lollipops. Cookies with Raisins That Look Like Chocolate Chips . . ."

"Ack!" said Circadia. "The Bad Dreams have even taken over the concession stand. Is nothing sacred?"

"This soda tastes like chlorine," said Dozer, who then tried a different flavor. "And this one tastes like . . . nose hairs? Spiders? How does a drink taste so . . . hairy?"

"I *am* fond of nougat," said Winks. "I suppose these Naked Nougats are just nougat without chocolate." He grabbed a few and popped them in his mouth.

"Look," I said, "I know we're all disappointed about these treats, but let's focus on the *reason* I called this meeting. Circadia and I discovered that this Essence of Murph can change someone into Murph. I mean, that's pretty amazing, right?"

"Um . . ."

"Uhhh . . ."

"Huh?" said the Dreamatics.

"And I've been giving it a lot of thought," I said. "And I . . . I volunteer to do it. To change into Murph."

"Dormir!" gasped Circadia. "You heard what the Memory Vault Keeper said. If someone turns into a memory by using Nostalgia . . . they stay that way. There's no turning back."

"I know," I said.

The Dreamatics all started talking and yelling out questions. Winks started crying.

"If someone—not necessarily you but someone—*were* to change into Murph," said Circadia, "what would we even do with them? Let the Bad Dreams make Murph Nightmares? Sounds awful."

"We do have that one-night-without-nightmares deal with Coco," I said. "We could perform that night."

"Perform what? A dream? Would that even help?" asked Dozer.

"Well, I've been thinking about it," I said, "and I'm pretty sure if we create a super-duper memorable dream, it will go into the Memory Bank. I mean, it's rare, but people remember dreams sometimes, right?"

"Yeah," said Circadia, getting excited, "and if Murph is back in the Memory Bank . . . then I bet Luna's other memories of Murph will come back!"

"Few questions," said Winks. "One: WHAT?! And two: How? And three: Does anybody feel a draft in here? I just got very cold."

"We could even base the dream on a memory. I recall

lots of Luna's memories," I said. "I figure we can all put our heads together, remember as much as we can, and then just . . . write the rest of it. We're creative. We're a great team."

"Correction," said Circadia, "we *were* a team. We're missing the Director, Nox, Tuck, Reverie, the Orchestra . . . They all fled when the Bad Dreams took over."

"Where are my shoes and socks?" said Winks. We all turned and looked at him.

"Um, they're on your feet," said Circadia.

"They most certainly are not," said Winks. "And my shirt! Who has taken my shirt!" He crossed his arms over his chest as if it was bare, even though he was still wearing his same silk and sequin cheetah-print top.

"I mean, I kind of *wish* your shirt would disappear," said Circadia, "since it hurts my eyes, but it's very much still on your body."

"Let's focus," I said, trying to ignore Winks. "We'll just have to find the rest of our team. Does anyone have any leads?"

"Reverie likes any reflective surface," said Dozer.

"Nox likes gardening and planting set seeds," said Circadia.

"And the Director said she needed a vacation," I added, "pretty much every day."

"I'M NOT WEARING ANY PANTS!" yelled Winks. "NOBODY LOOK AT MY KNEES!"

"Earlier today I did overhear one of the Bad Dreams,"

said Greeph, "speaking to another one about seeing, and I'm quoting them here, 'some weirdo getting a sunburn, screaming about seaweed, and complaining about sand fleas on the beach in set storage.'"

"That sounds like a theatre type," said Circadia. "Definitely one of us."

"Well, okay then," I said. "We'll start there."

And so we left the concession stand—with Winks wrapped in a blanket, convinced by the Naked Nougats he'd eaten that he was completely naked—and headed toward set storage and the smell of sunscreen, seaweed, and salty air.

Chapter Thirty-seven

SUNSCREENING MY SHELLEPHONE CALLS

"**M**y beach!" I shouted at the Director. "What have you done to my beautiful beach?!"

"I wasn't aware it was *your* beach," she replied, "but I consider it a vast improvement. Everything was so . . . chaotic before. Now just look at it."

"I am looking at it," I cried, "and it looks . . . it looks . . ."

"Controlled?" asked the Director. "Well-organized? Structured? Shipshape?" She was lounging in a beach chair near my sand fort, sipping a tropical drink, and wearing over her bathing suit a T-shirt that read *DON'T KRILL MY VIBE* with a picture of a small crustacean wearing sunglasses. There were several other T-shirts hanging on a clothesline behind her that read things like *I'M SUNSCREENING MY SHELLEPHONE CALLS, A VACATION? ALPACA MY BAGS* with a picture of a llama, *JUST DUNE MY THING,* and my personal least-favorite, *WISH YOU WEREN'T HERE.*

"This beach looks maniacally uptight," said Circadia. "Can a beach look uptight?"

"Did you . . . *direct* the beach?" asked Winks.

"What do you mean?" asked the Director.

"Well, you seem to have organized all the sand into piles—golden grains, white grains, crystal grains, pink grains. And the shells and pebbles are also sorted by type and color and shape. And the seaweed has been . . . washed and folded like clean laundry? And you've corralled all the crabs into some sort of small pen."

"I think you're missing the biggest change," I said, "which is that she *laid concrete* over the beach!"

"Isn't it great?" asked the Director. "It's so much easier to keep clean, and you don't get all that pesky sand all over the place, in your shoes and bathing suit."

"Do you think a coconut dropped on her head?" whispered Circadia into my ear.

"I heard that," said the Director, "and it did not. I'm on vacation, the first one in my *entire existence*, and it's *wonderfully* relaxing. I've been catching some waves, catching some Z's. Oh, is that the time?" she said frantically, looking at her watch. "Hold on just a moment, if we don't do our rehearsals on time, the Soft-shell Fabs get cranky."

Circadia and I looked at each other, and I knew she was thinking the same thing I was: *Do we even want to know who the Soft-shell Fabs are?*

"And a ONE, TWO, THREE, FOUR!" yelled the Director. At her feet sat a cardboard box that had been fashioned into a makeshift mini theatre, complete with seaweed curtains and a little driftwood stage. On it sat a group of crabs, all wearing tiny sequin top hats and holding little canes in their claws with various degrees of success.

"Clawde, you missed your cue!" yelled the Director. "Clawdia, watch your mark! Shelldon and Shellby, I said to make your way downstage, not upstage! Seamore, find your light! To your left, Mittens. No, your other left!"

Circadia slowly, slowly made her way toward the crab theatre and shut the curtains. Before the Director could protest, we both took her gently by the arms.

"Why don't we get you out of the sun?" said Circadia, looking up at the round globe lamp above us that was giving off amazingly realistic sunlight. "I know I made that, and it's not an actual sun, but I think it's definitely giving you heatstroke or brain boil or something. Shade is good, very good."

"I guess I could use a little break . . ." said the Director. "Crabs are even harder to work with than Reverie, if you can believe that."

Circadia and I both laughed. Perhaps our beloved Director wasn't totally gone after all.

After we all had a few cups of tea in my sandcastle fort—and a few minutes of the teakettle screaming facts about the ocean such as "IN A SURVEY THE SCARIEST SEA CREATURE NAMES WERE VAMPIRE SQUID, BLOB-FISH, GOBLIN SHARK, ZOMBIE WORMS, AND GIANT SQUID"—I got up the nerve to pitch my idea to the Director.

"We need you to direct a very memorable dream starring Murph the dog," I said. "But not really Murph—one of us playing Murph after we take a special potion. Well, more of an essence, and . . . um . . . yeah." I trailed off.

"Are you speaking to me?" asked the Director.

"Who else would he be talking to?" asked Circadia. "You are literally named *the Director*."

"Technically yes," said the Director, "but I've left that old life behind."

"So, what do we call you now?" asked Circadia.

"I mean, I'm still the Director," said the Director. "I don't want to go through all the effort and paperwork to change my name. But it's just a name now, not a *calling*."

"You should know," I said, "that things have gotten worse since you left. Luna has nightmares every night, and all her memories of Murph are missing, and if they don't come back, then eventually they'll be gone forever and the Bad Dreams will permanently take over the theatre.

"I feel sorry for Luna," said the Director. "I do. But I'm no longer in the business we call Show. My life now is a vacation—it's all about the call of the waves, about the sea and the sand."

"The sea and the concrete," corrected Circadia.

"What good is a vacation, if you don't have a real life to go back to?" I asked. "All refreshed and ready to dive back into your work? I mean, at a certain point, if you're always on vacation, do you really have a life at all?"

"That's a common misconception," said the Director, "but actually living on vacation is amazing and very relaxing. All I do is sort seashells and listen to tunes and sip drinks out of pineapples."

"That does sound nice," said Circadia.

"It really does," I said. "Maybe we should take a vacation."

"I know of a nearby beach with performing crabs," said the Director. "They're amateurs right now, but I think they could make it to the big time."

Circadia and I were both nodding dreamily when I realized the Director was casting her castaway spell on us too.

"No, NO!" I said. "You used to be the most dedicated Dreamatic of all. What happened? Where did all that passion go?"

The Director shrugged. "Out with the tide, I suppose."

That was it. The last straw. I knew what I had to do.

"Well, I guess that's that, then," I said. "We'll head back to the theatre. Hey, Circadia, which shirt do you think Coco will be wearing today? Maybe the one that has a picture of a carrot that says *KEEP CALM AND CARROT ON.*"

Circadia caught on right away. "Or the one with an otter floating on its back that says *YOU OTTER RELAX*," she added. "Or the one with a piece of cheese yelling *GOUDA RIDDANCE, STRESS!*"

"Yeah, Coco *loves* that one. Oooh, or maybe that one with a cheese grater that says *OH GRATE, IT'S MONDAY.*"

"Wait. Hold on. Stop. Halt," said the Director, closing her eyes and taking a deep, steadying breath. "That oafish, vulgar, ill-mannered, messy, unorganized, hulking mockery of a director is wearing *my* T-shirts?!"

"Oh yeah," I replied. "Every day. He's staining them with all the rotten food he eats and totally stretching out the arm and neck holes too."

"Even the one," said the Director, her voice quivering, "with a smiling pickle that says *MY JOB IS A BIG DILL?*"

"Yep. And even the one," I said, my voice low with warning, "with the goat and a text bubble saying *YOU GOAT THIS!*"

The Director got a look in her eyes that could only be described as a stormy sea. In the distance, an angry foghorn could be heard, like a ghost blowing its nose into the wind.

"Lights. Curtain. Places," said the Director, getting to her feet and looking out the fort toward the theatre. "Aaaaaand: Action. We've got a memorable dream to make and a theatre to save."

"Yes!" said Circadia and I, high-fiving.

"And some T-shirts to reclaim," continued the Director.

"It was a lot more inspiring without the last part," I said, "but sure. Okay. Let's go."

Chapter Thirty-eight

THE UNRELIABLE MAP

We studied the map on the wall in front of us, trying to figure out where the missing Dreamatics might be. The map showed all the places any of us knew to exist in or around the Lunarian Grand.

There was the theatre proper, with its stage, seats, orchestra pit, magical blinking curtain, and shape-changing statues.

There was the backstage area, with its dressing rooms, offices, the Pipe Dream, prop department, set department, costumes, weather closet, and the newly added New Wortehamfordshire.

There was the second-floor balcony, with its lighting booth, Daily Newsreel screening room, and thematically flavored popcorn.

There was the lobby with the self-changing marquee and concession stand.

There were the hallways wallpapered in playbills, the Department of . . . something . . . (the map had forgotten the name), and the Bottle of Scents Room.

There was prop storage with its candy forest, circus tents, ice garden, sleeping books, carriage moon, and insect carousel.

There was the (now paved) beach with my sandcastle fort and collection of treasures.

There was the Sub Floor with the Unseen Playwright's office.

There was the Map Room, which we stood in now, staring at the map of the Lunarian Grand. There were other maps, of course—a map of Luna's Known World (home, Lita's, school, the beach, the library, etc.), the Danger! Map (scary house down the street, Bermuda Triangle), the Best Reading Spots Map (under tree, in tree, in tent, window seat, back steps, hammock, in the closet), the Recurring Dream Locations Map (falling pit, classroom, weird version of Luna's house, car with nobody driving, museum, zoo, etc.), and so on.

"Where could they be?" I asked. "We've looked in every one of these places, and nothing, zip, zero Dreamatics."

"Well, not *everywhere*," said Circadia, pointing to the map.

The issue with the map of the Lunarian Grand, we soon discovered, was that it wasn't exactly a normal map. Because the Lunarian was so often redecorating and re-constructing itself on a whim, the map was . . . fairly unreliable. Just in the time we had been studying it, the map had changed the theatre's box seats, moved several cunning corridors and perfidious passageways, and added or removed several rooms that were labeled things like: the Improv Studio, the Lunar Library, the Snory Award Display Room, the Wandering Dark, the Newsreel Archives, the Office of Wishes, the Area Allegedly Haunted by Insomnia, and the room filled with Darkening Bugs (which were like lightning bugs, but the opposite).

The map also showed whatever weather was happening in the weather closet or elsewhere. Currently in the weather closet there were bursts of lightning and thunder, and when I put my hand over that area of the map, my fingers came away cold and wet with rain.

"It's an Unreliable Morpho-Map," said the Director.

"Interesting, but untrustworthy. I mean, just look at that corner at the top near the Bottle of Scents Room. It looks like it's been ripped away."

"Or bitten," said Circadia.

"Or just . . . missing," I whispered, knowing exactly where we needed to look next.

Chapter Thirty-nine

THE MISSING PART OF THE MAP SOCIETY

The missing part of the map was certainly not missing liveliness, that was for sure.

Dozer headed back to monitor the screening room and the rest of us made our way through the backstage and hallways, finally finding ourselves in what looked like a town square, complete with a fountain, trees, green grass, and one heavily leaning-to-the-left wooden building, a cat-shaped sign over the door that read, *THE MISSING PART OF THE MAP SOCIETY, MEMBERS ONLY*. As we entered, the cat sign hissed and slashed out a claw, then looked down at us quizzically, and finally lay down and started purring.

"I think we've been accepted to the society," said Circadia, "whatever that means."

Inside the building was a small café with music. Nobody seemed to be serving the beverages and pastries, but instead spoons stirred themselves in cups, and pastries rolled onto plates.

"Welcome, all Strays, Lost Things, and the Temporarily Misplaced," I read from the sign behind the coffee bar.

"This place . . ." said the Director, "it makes me feel adrift. Lost. Alone. Do you feel that? I feel like I'm in a boat in the middle of the sea, no land in sight, and nobody is searching for me."

"Look!" said Circadia. "It's some of the orchestra members. They're playing in a jazz trio up on the little stage."

Sure enough, there were a bass player, a trumpet player, and a saxophone player from the Forty Winks Orchestra.

"That explains my emotions," said the Director, "but not the décor."

She wasn't wrong. The interior had everything a normal café might—tables, chairs, a juice bar, some art on the walls—but every inch of everything was covered in hand-knit material. It all looked like it was meant to be made into scarves or blankets and instead covered the place like some sort of cozy, moss-like wrapping.

I stroked a brightly striped column. "Lovely," I said. "Very soft."

"Why thank you, Dormir," said a voice behind us. When I turned, I nearly fainted.

"Tuck, is it really you?" I asked, hugging him tightly.

Tuck! I thought. *Who made costumes that could make you breathe fire, costumes that could make you fly. Tuck! Our Tuck.*

"Since I wasn't designing costumes, I needed to do something with my restless fingers," he said. "So, I knitted a little outfit for, well, everything. It's no sequins glittering onstage, but it keeps me busy in this somewhat dispiriting place."

"Tell us *everything*," said Circadia. "What is this place? How'd you end up here?"

"We just wandered for a while and ended up here," said Tuck, "like we were drawn by an invisible magnet. Far as I can tell, it's where all of Luna's missing things go. A bunch of Dreamatics, sure, but also lots of other things. Up there, for example." He pointed to the ceiling. "See those little things flying around like moths attracted to the shadows? Those are Luna's High Spirits, clearly missing from her real life at the moment."

We all stared up, watching the moths bash their heads against the darkness instead of the light. Tuck pointed out other Missing Things to us as well: There were Little Happy Thoughts floating around like specks of dust in beams of sunlight, Jubilations crawling on the wall and blowing their little noisemakers, heart-shaped balloons called Light Heartednesses, and wee birds called Mirths and Merriments fluttering everywhere, their songs sounding like laughter.

"There are more outside," said Tuck. "And some other Dreamatics."

We all excitedly rushed outside, and sure enough, more Missing Things were there as well. There was a small pond in the center of the square, and on its surface frogs jumped from lily pad to lily pad, giggling instead of croaking.

"Luna's Lily-Laughters," explained Tuck.

But even more interesting than these was the figure leaning over the water, gazing at her own reflection.

"Oh, darling," she said to herself, "you look more beautiful today than yesterday. If you were a script, I would never want to be off book."

"Reverie?" said the Director. "Are you . . . okay?"

Reverie didn't seem to hear. "Are you opening night?" she continued, speaking to her reflection. "Because my heart flutters as you grow near."

"We may not be able to include Reverie in this endeavor," said the Director, patting her former star on the back.

"What I don't understand," I said, "is where all this came from. I mean, was there always a place for Missing Things here?"

"When we got here," said Tuck, "it was just the Members Only clubhouse. The rest of this was planted and grew up around it."

"You mean . . . Nox?" I asked.

"Did someone call for an out-of-work but world-class set designer?" said Nox, suddenly appearing, wiping her soil-covered gloves on her overalls, and giving each of us a very muddy hug.

"What are you doing here, Dormir?" she asked. "I honestly didn't think I'd ever see any of you again."

"It's a long story," I said. "But the gist of it is we're going to perform a memorable dream of Luna's that stars Murph, and we're going to put it into her Memory Bank with the help of the Early Bird and Night Owl Memory Vault Keepers, and then Luna will maybe, hopefully, be able to dream about Murph and remember him again."

"Not confusing at all," said Circadia.

"So, we have a Director," said the Director, "and sets, costumes, lights, music, an essence for an actor. But we're missing one very important ingredient."

"Popcorn?" asked Tuck.

"A fog machine?" asked Nox.

"A ghost named Insomnia that roams the theatre and haunts the lighting department?" asked Circadia.

"No," said the Director. "The Unseen Playwright is still missing, and we don't have a script. We need someone who knows these characters and memories inside out, better than they know themselves. Someone passionate, creative, with a love for comfortable workwear, a healthy dash of neurosis, and slightly low self-esteem. We need . . . *a writer.*"

I was racking my brain, trying to think of anyone who could fit that description, when I noticed that all the Dreamatics had gone quiet.

And had turned in the same direction.

And were smiling.

And were staring at *me.*

Chapter Forty

HAUNTED PENCILS

"I'm not qualified!" I protested as we all walked back toward the theatre from the missing part of the map. "Also, where would I lead this writers' room? I mean, we certainly can't use the Unseen Playwright's subterranean office, the ventilation alone is probably not safe, and furthermore—"

But it seemed, as always, the Lunarian Grand had taken care of everything; right beside the other offices was a new frosted-glass door with the words *THE WRITERS' ROOM* etched on it in bold black letters.

"Well, okay," I said, "sure, we have a *place* to write now, but that still doesn't make me qualified . . ."

As I spoke, the words *DORMIR: HEAD WRITER* appeared in slightly smaller font below *WRITERS' ROOM*.

"Does anyone else feel like this place possibly has too much attitude for a theatre?" I asked.

In reply, the words . . . *FOR NOW* appeared beside my name and title.

"Touché," I said.

The other Dreamatics and I began to investigate the space. There was a long wooden table with office chairs all around it, and at each seat was a pad of paper with the words MEMO(RY) PAD, a pencil, a glass, and pitcher of water. It was all very clean and crisp, exactly how I would have decorated a place. There were also little nameplates made of cardboard in front of the seats. They read:

DORMIR: HEAD WRITER
CIRCADIA: HUMOR
NOX: DIALOGUE
TUCK: ACTION
WINKS: PLOT TWISTS
THE DIRECTOR: YADA YADA YADA

The only decorations on the walls were large posters that looked like movie advertisements but depicted some of Luna's most memorable memories.

There was one of Luna and her family watching *101 Dalmatians*. At the bottom of the poster was a review quote: "Not enough dogs."—Murph. There was one of Murph as a puppy, wet and covered in a towel after he'd gotten confused on a rainy day and run to the neighbor's house instead of his own; the bottom of this poster read "Wet. Cold. Confusing plot."—Murph. There was a poster of the vacuum cleaner ("Evil. Scariest thing ever."—Murph), as well as a poster of the Roomba ("A truly evil sequel. Even scarier than the first!"—Murph), one of Murph's first time trying pizza ("Four paws up! How have I never experienced this before?"—Murph), Car ("10 MILLION STARS. BEST EVER!"—Murph), Walk ("10 BILLION STARS. BEST EVER!"—Murph), and finally a poster for Nose Kisses Before Bed, which was reviewed as "Lovely. Very relaxing. Made me sleepy, in a good way."—Murph.

I sighed. "Nose Kisses Before Bed—a timeless classic. I could watch it over and over."

"Really?" asked Circadia. "Of these, I liked Roomba the best. A killer robot! Pew, pew! Or whatever it does—I'm still not totally sure. Laser zaps dust?"

"Ahem," said the Director, clearing her throat and nodding at me.

"Oh, right," I said. "I can't just goof around with my friends. I'm, um, in charge in here. Okay . . . well, let's see. How about we go around and each say our name and one fun fact about ourselves."

"We've literally all known one another since we existed," said Tuck. "Respectfully."

"True, true," I said. "Okay, instead, why don't you all write down your favorite Murph memory."

There was some mumbling—I can only assume about how horribly I was doing as a head writer—but then everyone started writing. Circadia laughed as she wrote, Winks looked shocked, and Nox and Tuck seemed rather bored. But the Director looked completely confused, crumpling notebook sheets, and starting over and over again.

"Everything okay, Director?" I asked.

"Definitely not," she said. "I want to write about the memory where Murph went to the pet store for the first time and got to pick out any toy in the place, but every time I try, all that comes out is blather."

"Let me see," I said, and she handed me her latest sheet of paper.

It was morning when they entered the pet shop, the light flowing through the windows in beams of sunshine, illuminating the faces of the various toys—squeaky pigs, floppy-eared bunnies, and a whole wall of spherical sheep—each wishing, hoping, wondering if today would be the day, the one when they'd be chosen to go home with that special pup.

"Yeah, this has nothing to do with Murph," I said. "Total filler. Could I see your pencil?"

The Director handed it over and I studied it. It looked like a totally normal yellow pencil with an eraser, except on the side it said *YADA YADA YADA PENCIL*. I tried using the pencil to write down one of my own favorite memories, but instead of writing what I intended, the pencil wrote:

As Luna kissed Murph's nose, she thought about how it possesses up to three hundred million olfactory receptors, compared to about six million in humans. And that the part of a dog's brain that is devoted to analyzing smells is about forty times larger than a human's. And that dogs also have neophilia, which means they are attracted to new, exciting, and interesting odors.

"It's like this pencil has a mind and mission of its own," I said.

"THE PENCILS ARE CLEARLY HAUNTED!" shouted Winks, putting his cape over his face.

"It's true," said Circadia. "No matter what I want to write, it comes out really funny. Like, I wanted to write about the Roomba memory, but instead the pencil wrote:

'Question: In what order does the Roomba vacuum the house? Answer: Roomba room.'"

"Well, your name card does say *Humor*, and that was marginally funny," said Nox. "If it helps, my pencil is haunted too."

"I don't think we've concluded that the pencils are, in fact, haunted," I said.

"I was writing a simple sentence about Luna and Murph's favorite movie," continued Nox, "and the pencil made it look like this." Nox held up his pad to show us all.

PONGO THE DALMATIAN
Lucky! Patch! Pepper! Freckles!
And Rolly, you little rascal!

"Pretty snappy dialogue," said Circadia.

"It's from *101 Dalmatians*," said Nox. "But I wasn't *trying* to write dialogue."

Tuck informed us that his pencil only wrote action, and Winks said that his only wrote completely shocking things.

"My pencil is very melodramatic!" said Winks. "Everything I write with it sounds like some sort of soap opera or murder mystery. I mean, *What are we going to do? How are we going to write this script?* THIS IS CLEARLY THE END OF THE WORLD!"

"Are you entirely sure it's the pencil in your case?" asked Circadia.

The Dreamatics all began arguing amongst themselves, while I walked around inspecting the pencils. They each looked as normal as the last. I sighed, picked up Winks's pencil, and wrote a note to myself to find new pencils. Except it didn't exactly come out that way. Instead, it read:

MY FIRST DAY AS HEAD WRITER AND WE'RE POSITIVELY BEWITCHED BY HAUNTED PENCILS! WHAT'S GOING TO HAPPEN NEXT? WOE IS ME! THE HORROR! THE HORROR! DUM, DUM, DUUUUUM!!

Chapter Forty-one

INSIDE THE WRITERS' ROOM

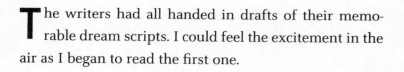

The writers had all handed in drafts of their memorable dream scripts. I could feel the excitement in the air as I began to read the first one.

<u>ACT ONE</u>

EXT. THE BEACH—MORNING

A GIRL stands on the beach. She is totally still, face turned toward the sky as if waiting for something.

The sky is peach pie with à la mode clouds, fading to a chocolate raspberry rhapsody.

GIRL
(whispering)
There you are . . .

A single snowflake falls very slowly from the
sky, one of those fat, fluffy ones. It's majestic. It's
calming. It's beautiful.

The snowflake has the distinct feeling that it's
special—not trophy-winning special or rock
star special, but truly one of a kind. No matter
how many billions of snowflakes fall from the
sky, there are never two the same.

Suddenly a young DOG flies into the scene, leaps
into the air, and eats the snowflake. More flakes
start falling, and the dog tries his best, to no
avail, to eat them all.

The girl puts her arms and face toward the sky
and begins turning in circles, dancing in
the snow.

GIRL

Did you remember to turn off
the stove?

DOG

(barks)

GIRL

I don't remember if I remembered to
turn off the stove. It's interesting, this
beach is actually starting to feel
like a stove . . .

As suddenly as the snow started, it stops and
sun breaks through the clouds. Hot sun. The
beach becomes a tropical oasis, complete with
swaying palm trees, fruity drinks, and the smell
of sunscreen and orange blossoms fills the air.

I put down the script page I'd been reading, then
picked it up again, then put it down.

"Um, Director," I said, "did you happen to write this
using your Yada Yada Yada pencil?"

"Yes, what else would I use?" She sighed. "Literally,
those are the only pencils in here."

"Because," I continued, trying to be delicate with my
criticism, "it's reading a tad . . . like it's filled with filler.
A bit . . . pointless. And finally, what exactly happened
there at the end? Palm trees and fruity drinks?"

"I'm still on vacation time," the Director said with a
shrug, putting on a pair of sunglasses.

"Okey dokey," I said. "Let's move onto the next attempt.
Winks? Let's see what you wrote."

ACT ONE

EXT. THE BEACH—MORNING

A GIRL stands on the beach. She is totally still,
face turned toward the sky as if waiting for something. She is wearing a stunning designer jump-
suit with a rhinestone belt and chic feathered hat.

GIRL

UP THERE! SO MAJESTIC! AHHHH!!

A single snowflake falls very slowly from the sky.

A DOG saunters into the scene and eats the
snowflake. He dances on his back legs trying to
eat all the falling flakes. The dog is wearing an
iridescent collar with jewels.

GIRL

YES, DANCE WITH THE SNOW. FEEL IT
IN YOUR BONES! FEEL THE RHYTHM!

The girl puts her arms and face toward the sky
and begins turning in circles, dancing in the snow.

Suddenly there's a rumbling from the hills
above. The snow on the mountains begins to
crumble away, until . . .

EVERYONE ON THE BEACH

It's an avalanche! RUN FOR YOUR LIVES!

The avalanche is about to hit when a dashing
young STRANGER runs onto the scene.

DASHING YOUNG STRANGER

I know we JUST MET and I don't know
your name, but . . .
I LOVE YOU.

He is about to kiss the girl when the avalanche covers them in snow.

The dog, now wearing a stylish rescue jacket and low-heeled boots, digs through the snow to rescue them both.

Once again the girl and young stranger are about to share a kiss when . . .

ALL OF THEIR TEETH FALL OUT!

"Wow!" I said.

"Why, thank you," said Winks, taking a dramatic bow, "thank you very much."

"I did not mean that *wow* in a good way."

"Ouch," said Winks.

"I'm sorry," I said, "that wasn't constructive of me. What I mean is: Why is everyone yelling? Where did the avalanche come from? And Luna has never even *had* her first kiss!"

"I just felt the scene needed some melodrama," said Winks. "Some romance. Some PIZZAZZ"

I nodded. "Right, but none of this happened. Especially not the ending, where everyone loses their teeth. I suppose we can blame your pencil too?"

"No," said Winks. "I actually misplaced my pencil before writing this."

I sighed loudly.

"Tuck," I said, "you've got a great imagination. You must have come up with a script that's interesting but also true to Luna's memory, right? Let's see it."

ACT ONE

EXT. THE BEACH—MORNING

A GIRL stands on the beach. She is totally still, face turned toward the sky as if waiting for something.

A single snowflake falls slowly from the sky. She smiles at it.

A DOG enters the scene, leaping through the air and eating the snowflake. He begins spinning in circles, jumping, trying to eat all the snowflakes that are now falling.

The girl puts her arms and face toward the sky and begins turning in circles, dancing in the snow.

Out on the sea, a sailboat passes by, the name S.S. DREAMBOAT printed on the side.

On the boat, a group of Dreamatics has an out-door tea party, the snowflakes flavoring their drinks like bits of sugar.

The girl on the beach puts her out her hand, and each time an individual snowflake lands on her skin, she can feel the memory of where it came from before it was up in a cloud and then became snow: One flake started as water that cradled a bog creature; another was a healing tear from a Phoenix; one was water from a broken snow globe; and another, evaporated liquid from inside a witch's cauldron. One flake was once seawater flicked off the end of a mermaid's tail; and one was dog drool, dribbled out during a most wonderful dream.

The girl and dog find seashells on the beach together, the kind that swirl and curl into themselves and, if put to an ear, can sound of a distant sea. But when the girl puts the shell to her ear, she can also hear the gulls and the whale song and the chirping of dolphins.

"I . . . don't remember any of that happening," I said, awestruck. "I mean, it was good. Interesting. Wild. But very, very inaccurate. Also, why is there no dialogue?"

"Oh," said Tuck, "the pencil let me write what I wanted, but only the action parts."

"Of course," I said. "Well, Circadia, my brilliant bestie, I know you won't let me down. What did you come up with?"

ACT ONE

EXT. THE BEACH—MORNING

A GIRL stands on the beach. She is totally still, face
turned toward the sky as if waiting for something.
Snow falls on the beach, and the girl and her
DOG try to catch the flakes, she with her hands,
the dog with his mouth.

> GIRL
> Here's one for you: Where did the dog go
> on vacation?

> DOG
> (stares blankly)

> GIRL
> New Yorkie City!

> DOG
> (stares blankly)

> GIRL
> What did the Dalmatian say after eating dinner?

> DOG
> (stares blankly)

> GIRL
> Boy, that really hit the spot!

DOG

(stares blankly)

GIRL

What do you call a dog who works as

a magician?

DOG

(stares blankly)

GIRL

A Labracadabrador!

DOG

(stares blankly)

I admit, I started to cry a little at this point.

"But . . . how . . . and why . . . and what even—"

"Well, I tried to write the real memory!" said Circadia. "The one with the seashell they found. But every time I put my pencil to the page. . ."

"Your humor pencil just wrote whatever it wanted," I said. "Of course. Well, last but not least is Nox, who has the dialogue pencil. So this should be . . . exhausting."

ACT ONE

EXT. THE BEACH—MORNING

A GIRL stands on the beach. She is totally still, face turned toward the sky as if waiting for something.

Snow falls, and the girl and her DOG try to catch the flakes.

NARRATOR (Offstage)

It was Murph the dog's first snow. I mean, the first snow he got to go outside and see and play in up here in Massachusetts. I guess he was born in Mississippi? But who knows—do dogs have birth certificates or something like that? All I know is that sometimes when Luna would pretend to speak in Murph's voice, she'd often give him a Southern accent. Though other times it was British, so your guess is as good as mine? The beach, though! Wait, which beach was it? Was it Herring Cove or Long Point? Oh, duh, it was probably the dog beach. And half of it was white with snow, but just up to the seaweed line where the waves and tide would come in, and that part was still sand. It was like a before and an after—like if you walked in the sandy part it was still summer, and then if you crossed the line it was suddenly winter. And the sun was just touching the sandbar, which was covered in seagull prints like ancient hieroglyphics. It was like in that movie—you know, the one, with the woman, from the other movie, with all the ghosts? She actually looks a lot like Luna's cousin . . . well, I think it might actually be her

second cousin, but I never really understood
what that meant. Oh, and SHE was quite a
character; worked as a sea captain but secretly—
don't tell anyone—never learned to swim!

"I just . . . we need help," I said.

Everyone else nodded, including the characters in
the posters on the walls. I dropped my head down onto
the table.

"Also," I added, "I think it goes without saying, but I'll
be confiscating all the haunted pencils."

Chapter Forty-two

LIKE AN OCTOPUS, WE CONTAIN SEVERAL HEARTS

The next morning, I found myself overseeing my first ever writers' retreat. I'd prepared several writing exercises and lessons and began the day by reading from *The Dreamweaver's Handbook.*

"A dream, or *Somnium Imaginatio,*" I read, "is part of an order that includes daydreams, naps, lucid dreams, hopes, wishes, and longings. While Dreams originated in Amygdala, they now occur throughout most of the world in fresh water, salt water, equatorial, and sub-polar emotional climates alike. Dreams have virtually no predators, with the noted exception of Insomnia.

"Nope, absolutely not," I said, slamming the book shut. "No speaking of Insomnia. Not on my watch. Winks," I continued, "you mentioned you had a game we could play to work on our ability to write characters?"

Winks jumped up with joy, and began his game, but things did not go as planned.

"Nice to meet you, I'm a penguin," said Circadia.

"And I'm . . . a bowl of soup," replied Tuck.

"No, no, NO!" shouted Winks, who was flailing with frustration. "This is called 'Meet and Greet,' and the way to play is that everyone walks around the room, and any time you bump into someone, you introduce yourself as a new person with *specific* details about who you are."

"Ah," said Tuck. "In that case: Pleasure to meet you, Penguin, I am a bowl of New England clam chowder."

"Ugh!" said Winks. "No, you introduce yourself IN CHARACTER. It's an ACTING exercise. How are you going to ACT like a BOWL OF SOUP?!"

I had hoped the game would help with our writing, but all it had accomplished thus far was that Winks was now hyperventilating into a paper bag, and everyone else was arguing whether a bowl of soup would act feverish or afraid to be eaten.

"Why don't we just try to do an improv scene," I suggested. "In Luna's drama club, improv is where you perform a little scene without a script. You just make it up as you go along, often from a suggested scenario. The only rules are: Be honest, listen, and embrace a 'yes' mind-set. Circadia and the Director, why don't you two start us off. Does anyone have a suggestion for the scene?"

"GETTING A HAIRCUT YOU HATE!"

"TWO PEOPLE HAVE THE SAME DREAM AND TELL EACH OTHER!"

"SOUP!"

"Okay," I said, "I heard two people both having the same dream. Aaaaaand ACTION!"

"Last night I dreamed of a giant marshmallow," said Circadia.

"Me too," said the Director. "Did you try to eat it? I did."

"Me too," said Circadia. "I ate the whole thing. But when I woke up . . ."

Circadia looked to me, unsure. I did a "keep going" motion with my hand.

"When I woke up . . ." continued Circadia, "my pillow was gone."

Everyone burst out laughing.

"You did it!" I yelled. "Improvved your improvement! Er, you improved our improv! Up next . . . a poetry writing workshop with a special guest instructor."

*   *   *

Greeph sat on a stool, the rest of us in a circle of chairs around him. He was wearing sunglasses, a scarf, and a fedora. In his hands was a leather-bound journal and fountain pen.

"Poetry. Prose. Literature," he said, lowering his sunglasses. "These are what we will explore in today's writing workshop. I will teach you how to toil, and edit, and

217

toss away. And then sometimes, briefly, what you're writing will no longer be just words, and will become every beautiful thing—the smell of fresh rain, the light of a porch lamp back home, the hollow call of geese pointing their arrow passed us all and onward to infinite summer."

"That's lovely," said Winks, wiping a tear. "I want to go with the geeses."

"Well then, let's get to work," smiled Greeph. "One of the keys to writing is to identify an emotion. For example, with the geese, what is the emotion it brings up?"

"The passage of time," I said quietly.

"And how nothing, no matter how beautiful, can last forever," added Circadia.

"Wonderful," said Greeph. "Now I want you each to write a sentence where you make that emotion into a thing; something tangible and solid, like the geese. Try to make it unexpected, make it our own. Write it down and put it in this hat."

Greeph stood up and placed his fedora onto the stool.

And so, we did what Greeph asked: We wrote about what we loved, what broke our hearts, and the color of the light when it happened. We tried to make these things solid, so someone else could pick them up off the surface of things, understand their shape and weight. When we were finished, Greeph took the hat, mixed up our sentences, then laid them out in a random order.

"I call this," he said, "'Our Poem,' and when I read it, you won't be able to tell who wrote which lines."

He read:

Like an octopus, we contain several hearts, one to keep, some to walk around outside us

The light off a face so well-known that it's a shock to see a new freckle, spot, scar

When flowers bow their heads in the vase, but it feels too soon for them to be gone

The sound a rusty bike makes, crying its reddish-brown coppery tears

The way the light of the sky looks, when looking up from the bottom of a pool or pond

The ocean at sunset, a sea of honey holding wax ships sailed by bees

It hurts, but it will always run through you, one of the most important threads

The toy from summer, much chewed, left outside to look lost in the cold winter

The electric white light of new snow, so bright you must close your eyes to see

The light through a thin book page, the shadow of a hand behind ready to turn

"That last line," said Circadia, "it's like a goodbye."

"It's beautiful," agreed Greeph. "I'm very proud of you all."

I thought about goodbyes.

Soon, it would be my last day at the theatre. How hard was it going to be to say goodbye to my friends? I knew that nothing lasts forever, so there would always be infinite goodbyes in life. And what was the alternative? *Not* getting to say goodbye? Like Luna and Murph? I'd seen from Luna that the absence of a goodbye just meant there was a hole that would never be filled, a phantom conversation that never got to be spoken, roaming the halls of the heart.

Suddenly, a lightbulb turned on above my head.

A thought fluttered around it like a moth.

Luna never got to say goodbye to Murph.

How could she? Murph was gone.

Except, not exactly.

Because she had the Lunarian Grand, the Dreamatics, and one lowly-low assistant-turned-head-writer who was prepared to become Murph for her.

"Everyone," I said to my writers, "I know how to rewrite the script."

Chapter Forty-three

THE COUNTING SHEEP

I thought after our successful writing workshops that things would go smoothly.

I thought after we had worked together to rewrite a new, fantastic script (which we did after the workshops! It was great!) that things would be easier. Rehearsals would go swimmingly. The production of the new memory would be a breeze.

And why did I think these things? Because I am a fool, and basically wrong about everything.

"Why does the snow keep changing to feathers?" I asked.

Nox just stared at the feathers falling from the rafters as if they were alien beings.

"I got snow from the weather closet," he said. "Just regular . . . snow . . ."

"You have to admit," said Circadia, "it's better than the baked potatoes."

It had, in fact, snowed baked potatoes before the feathers. And before the baked potatoes, it had snowed ladybugs. And before the ladybugs it had snowed yellow Post-it notes, each one printed with a single word: "BAAA."

"Honestly," said the Director, who was supposed to be directing but was instead sitting in a lounge chair on the beach set, "I think we should be more worried about this ocean. I mean, what even is this? It's totally dampening my vacay vibes. And it smells like . . . cinnamon?"

I looked at the back of the set, where Nox had built a realistic ocean fading into the distance. Except where before it had looked like blue-green water and crashing waves, it now looked like . . .

"It's milk," said Circadia, tasting the now-white ocean. "And a sort of sugary cinnamon-covered cereal. It's actually delicious."

The ocean, like the snow, then proceeded to changed again—from cereal and milk to marinara sauce, and then to butterscotch pudding.

"WHAT IS EVEN HAPPENING?" I yelled at nobody in particular.

"If I may," said Winks. "I think the trouble we're running into could have something to do with emotions. We're probably getting some central truth wrong, and the theatre knows it."

"Well, what should we do?" I asked.

"There's only one thing we can do," said Winks. "Make a visit to the Counting Sheep."

"No!" shouted Circadia.

"Anything but that!" yelled Tuck.

"The horror! THE HORROR!" screamed Winks.

"It was your idea," I said to him.

"I know," he gasped, "but *still,* ick, no thanks."

*　　*　　*

The Counting Sheep were not particularly popular among the Dreamatics.

Their department was all about crunching numbers, which was contrary to our whole artistic vibe as makers of dreams. The sheep kept watch on the technical side of Luna's dreams, and especially to figure out the timing of Luna's sleep—her light, deep, and REM cycles. Their offices were filled with rows and rows of desks with huge typewriters on top (the keys were extra large: for hooves). At each desk sat a sheep dressed in office attire—mostly smart skirts and blazers or suits and bow ties.

"Can I help you?" asked the sheep receptionist when I entered the office.

"I'm Dormir. Head writer of the current memorable dream in production starring Murph the dog. We're having some issues at rehearsals."

"The fact is," said the receptionist, with more than a hint of condescension, "that Murph the dog is no longer with us. He's beyond the veil. Taking the big sleep. Gone to a better place. He's at the big dog park in the sky. He joined the choir invisible. He took his last bow."

"I'm *aware,* sir," I said to the sheep. "Is there perhaps someone else I could speak to about this matter?"

"DENISE!" yelled the receptionist.

"It's Bernice, actually," said a nearby sheep, pushing up her horn-rimmed glasses with her hoof.

"Denise," said the receptionist, "I need you to—" POOF! The receptionist disappeared into thin air.

"Of course," I said, sighing. "Classic Counting Sheep."

"I'm sure he'll be right back," said Bernice. "I'm Denise, by the way."

"I thought it was *Bernice . . .*"

"Oh, right." Bernice laughed. "So, what can I—" And POOF! She disappeared as well.

"THIS IS WHY NOBODY LIKES COMING HERE," I said (to nobody).

After a minute or two, the receptionist and Bernice both reappeared, out of breath. Bernice's glasses were askew and she had bits of grass stuck to her skirt and coat.

"I almost sprained my ankle, I think," said the receptionist. "Was the fence taller tonight or what? What does she think, we're Olympic sheep?! How is me plummeting to my death over a too-high fence going to relax Luna and help her fall asleep? I mean *come on.*" Then he noticed me. "Oh, you're still here. Denise, help this Dreamatic, will you? I'm going on break."

"Hi again," said Bernice. "Pardon our disappearance."

"So, what's it like disappearing to be counted all the time?" I asked as we walked toward Bernice's office. The sign on her door read *DREAM DATA.*

"Well, it's not all the time," said Bernice, "just when Luna can't sleep and tries counting sheep. It's not so bad. Nice bit of exercise between crunching the numbers. I keep tennis shoes under my desk just for nights like this when Luna is restless."

The sheep kicked off her heels and laced up the sneakers.

"But a Dreamatic!" she continued. "Now *that's* interesting work. How can I help?"

"We wrote a script and are rehearsing a memory and—" But before I could finish, POOF! Bernice vanished once again.

"Well, at least she put on her comfy shoes," I said with a sigh, settling in for another wait while Luna counted her sheep.

When Bernice returned, I assaulted her with words.

"Let me just ask you really quickly before you leave again," I said, speaking a mile a minute, "we're trying to rehearse a dream to put in the Memory Bank to help Luna get back her Murph memories, but every time we do the sets go bonkers and the snow turns to meatballs or the ocean turns to guacamole, and your department is all about facts and details, so can you please help us figure out what is going on, thanks!"

I handed Bernice our script and she read it over, making little checkmarks in the margins.

"All looks okay to me," said Bernice. "Let me ask you, what filter are you using?"

"Circadia is in charge of lighting," I said, "and since this dream is based in part on a memory that takes place on the beach at sunset, she's using a big spotlight shaped like a conch shell that glows peachy pink."

"That's likely your issue right there," said Bernice. "A memory-based dream can be different from the wild dreams you're used to producing. A memory has facts, yes, but it also has emotions. Those are all Luna's, and not only are they specific to her, but they can change at different times. The memory of a favorite meal, for example, can become tarnished if one time it gives you food poisoning. The memory of a favorite doll can become tarnished if it ends up coming to life and, say, attacking you."

"Grim," I replied. "So, the memory of a memory can be . . . tainted? Polluted?"

"Yes. And then it can change tints again, or change back to the original," said Bernice. "You need to find the right filter for this memory at *this* time in order for your performance to work. Let me ask you a very important question: What is Luna's emotional state *right now*?"

Chapter Forty-four
MADAME GRIMELDA TELLS YOUR FORTUNE

Back in the screening room, Dozer was dozing, and the Daily Newsreel was about to begin. I could guess at Luna's emotional state—judging by the number of sheep she was counting in an effort to sleep—but perhaps a miracle had happened. Maybe she'd won the lottery or the Pulitzer Prize while we'd been gone. Though, the more I thought about it, I wasn't even sure those things would cheer her at this point.

"It's starting," called Dozer, sitting up in his seat like he'd heard an internal alarm clock.

Circadia and I got some popcorn (lasagna-flavored, strangely good), and settled into our seats. We heard the music that always started the Daily Newsreel, and then watched the highlights of Luna's day: At school she was given a caterpillar in a plastic container that would soon go into its cocoon, for dinner there was lasagna (which explained the popcorn flavor), and after that Luna's dads watched a movie about the end of the world while Luna went upstairs, saying she had a headache, but really just wanting to be alone.

"But Luna *loves* disaster movies," I said, munching my popcorn. "Volcanoes. Giant insects. Asteroids. It's very unlike her to miss a new one."

In her room, Luna was surrounded by her own disastrous mess. There were papers on every surface, and just as many tacked to every inch of the wall, some with large question marks written on them in bright marker.

"What's she doing?" I asked Dozer. "Solving a crime?"

"Not sure," he said, "but she's been at it for a few nights now."

As Luna studied the scraps of paper, I did too. At first, they didn't seem connected, but then I realized what we were looking at.

"Those are sketch ideas," I said, "for *The Luna and Murph Ten-Minutes-After-Dinner-and-Not-a-Moment-Longer Show*. Remember? They wanted to call it *The Luna and Murph Variety Hour,* but it turned out the audience of her dads could only handle ten minutes."

"I forget," said Circadia. "Why are they written mostly on napkins? Did she run out of paper?"

"No," I said, "it's just because she came up with most

of the sketches while they were eating dinner. Those nap-kins are collector's items!"

"Oh, right," said Circadia. "Now I remember that great bit where she'd say, 'My dog has no nose!' and her dad would say, 'How does he smell?' And she would say, 'TERRIBLE.' "

Circadia and I laughed. Not just because it was a solid joke, but also because every time she told it, Murph always looked offended, right on cue.

Now on the Newsreel, we watched as Luna snatched up a drawing of a circular ball sitting on some kind of stand. Luna studied it as if she was trying to figure something out.

"I know what that is," I whispered. "I know what she's looking for."

"What?" asked Circadia.

"Madame Grimelda," I said.

"Ooooooh," said Circadia.

"Aaaaah," said Dozer.

"That's exactly what Madame Grimelda would have said," I replied, and smiled as I remembered the first time Madame Grimelda had appeared on the Luna and Murph show.

Luna had been wearing a wig and a sparkly cape that had come with her magic set. Murph had on a bedazzled bandana, clip-on earrings, and a look of surrender. They both tried their best to appear as if they were communing with spirits beyond—Luna by swaying back and forth and waving her hands over her crystal ball (which was really a snow globe), and Murph by destroying a toy and sending it to the spirit realm.

"Oh hello!" said Luna. "It is I, Madame Grimelda. I am a psychic, and this is my familiar." She motioned to Murph. "I'm here today because I heard it was your birthday, Mr. Matías, and I'm going to tell your fortune. Let us look into the crystal ball."

Luna removed the cloth covering her snow globe with a flourish. "Oooh," she said, "ahhhh."

She stroked the snow globe as if it were a pet she was convincing to tell her its secrets. "Let us look to your future . . . hmmm, yes, I see pickles . . . I see cheese . . . I see *you* . . . ah yes, all things that are aging well!"

Luna's dads both laughed and clapped. Murph, who had finished eating his toy, placed his head on her lap.

"It seems my familiar has had a vision as well," she said, leaning down so Murph could whisper his witchy secrets into her ear. "Mmhmm," she said. "Oh, yes. My familiar tells me he sees things that are beginning to click . . . yes, things in your life are beginning to click . . . OH WAIT . . . that would actually be your knees, your elbows, and your hips . . . because you are forty-one."

At this, Luna's dad Ted nearly spit out the birthday carrot cake he was eating with a burst of laughter.

"What else?" said Luna, looking into her ball. "I see

hairs . . . growing in strange places and needing to be plucked . . . I see you trying to pull off sideburns . . . I see your daughter. Ah yes, she wishes you feliz cumpleaños, a most beautiful day, and no, the sideburns aren't working. And what's that?"

Luna leaned down as if Murph was talking into her ear once again.

"Yes, and my familiar has predicted that you are going to give him the rest of your cake."

I pulled my attention from the memory to the present-day Newsreel, where Luna had found the piece of paper she was looking for—the one with the Grimelda scene written on it—and was now setting up a circle of tennis balls and Milk-Bones on the bathroom floor. Luna had put on her wig and glitter cape. In front of her she placed her snow globe and several lit tealight candles. Finally, and with some difficulty, she wrangled her neighbor's twin cats into the bathroom as well. Normally Toil and Trouble liked Luna since she would sometimes catsit for them, but forcing them into a small bathroom with lit candles seemed a bridge too far even for them, and they began yowling at the door.

"What's she doing now?" asked Circadia. "Having a picnic?"

"No," I replied, "a séance. I think Luna—er, Madame Grimelda—is going to try and reach her familiar on the other side."

We watched Luna take out a homemade Ouija board. It had the usual two rows of letters, and a *yes* and a *no* in the two top corners, but it also had the words *TREAT, WALK, GOOD,* and *BAD.* There was a hand-drawn border of paw prints, and in place of the usual little triangle glass window thing players moved with their fingers, Luna had placed in the center of the board a Milk-Bone with an arrow drawn on it.

"Does Murph know how to spell out messages?" asked Circadia.

"Their bond clearly transcends language," I replied.

"Listen," Luna said to Toil and Trouble, "I read that some dog owners report hearing their dog's toenails clicking against the hardwood floor long after the pet has died. Some owners have felt the weight of their dog lying at their feet or beside them in bed."

She paused, the cats staring back at her. "I mean, I haven't. But maybe I could."

The cats yowled in response.

"I know this isn't your favorite activity, but whoever heard of having a séance alone? So I need your help. Let's do it for Murph, okay?"

Who knows if it was the pep talk or that the cats had just become resigned to capture, but they both flopped down beside the board and Luna was able to put a hand on Toil and close their little circle. With her other hand, she placed two fingers on the Milk-Bone.

"Murph . . . are you there?" asked Luna. "Can you hear us?"

Nothing.

Circadia, Dozer, and I all joined hands as well.

"Murph," said Luna, "it's me. I just . . . I just think I'd feel better if I knew you were kind of around, you know? Like if you were watching over us or something like that, our watchdog angel or something. I don't even have to see you, I just want to know you're there. I think then I could be okay and everything wouldn't feel so totally wrong. It's too quiet, and none of the furniture is covered in fur. Even your smell is starting to go away."

Still nothing.

"Murph?" asked Luna one last time, her closed eyes starting to spill over with tears. "I miss you. Can you talk to me? Please?"

I sat there, my pulse pounding, sure that at any moment Murph's ghost would move the Milk-Bone. Suddenly, there was movement in the room—a thumping noise. I let out a small yelp.

"Murph?" I whispered at the same time as Luna.

"The Milk-Bone is moving," said Luna.

We all watched expectantly, ready to see the Milk-Bone pointing to *GOOD* or the letter *M* for *Murph*.

But the thump we'd heard was Toil breaking the séance circle to hop onto the windowsill and search for escape, and the movement of the Ouija board was Trouble trying to inspect the Milk-Bone, getting too close to the candle, and singeing the end of her tail.

The séance was over.

If Murph was present, he was certainly having a good laugh.

But at least I now knew the current emotions of Luna, and maybe, just maybe, I could find the perfect lens through which to make our dream memory feel just right.

Chapter Forty-five

THE OFF-KILTER
FILTER

Now that we knew Luna's emotional state—when we last saw her she was lying on the bathroom floor, her cheek against the cold tile like when she had a stomach bug—we could hopefully find the right emotional filter for our memory performance and get our show on the road.

Or at least that's what we would have done if the Lunarian Grand hadn't been beaten down and broken in our absence.

"What have you done *now*?" I asked the Bad Dreams. Several of them were clawing the beaded eye curtains, shredding them like old rags. "Those are *magical dream curtains,* not your dirty underpants being kicked into the hamper!"

The Bad Dreams had also put hideous linoleum tiles over the theatre's handsome wooden floors, replaced the seats with vinyl massage chairs, and they'd even drawn devilish eyebrows, mustaches, and beards on all the playbills.

I noticed several walls had been knocked out and new doors installed along the back of the theatre. They had signs with things like *INSULTS ROOM, DOWNWARD SPIRAL,* and *FALLING OVER AND OVER ROOM.* Classic Bad Dreams kind of stuff.

I looked around the theatre, a place I suspected held secrets I still couldn't fathom. So why was it allowing the Bad Dreams to tear it apart? They were completely ruining the place, yet the theatre was no longer protesting. What was going on? Was the Lunarian losing its powers for good . . . or giving up?

The thought sent goose bumps over my skin, and I moved to press my face against the cold, smooth wood of the theatre wall. I laid my hands against the wall too, and stayed there for quite some time, breathing slowly and taking comfort in the closeness of my old friend. The theatre had always been so strong and sturdy, but the wood felt hollow against my palms—the whole place felt ashamed, weak, and broken. I listened to see if the theatre would tell me any secrets. When it didn't, I went ahead and just asked.

"Why did you stop fighting back?" I whispered.

I listened for a few minutes more but didn't hear anything, so I sighed and pulled away. When I did, I was surprised to find that the wall I'd just been leaning against was now a hallway—a cunning corridor or perfidious passageway for sure—and it was clear that the Lunarian wanted me to walk into it and exit to locations unknown.

I did, of course. If you ask a building a question and it tries to answer you, it's only polite to listen.

The hallway was dim, lit only by flickering candles in sconces along the walls. As I walked by, they seemed to cast strange shadows on the walls, each one taking shapes I recognized—shapes of my own fears and longings and dreams I thought were mine and mine alone. They disappeared as quickly as they'd blinked by, and I rubbed my eyes.

"Probably just seeing things," I mumbled.

At the end of the twisty hallway, I was delivered to a location backstage that I knew well. It was the spot where I used to stand to feed Reverie her lines. Often during rehearsals or scenes, there'd be long lulls, and I would read all the names and quotes carved into the wooden wall. Every Dreamatic had signed the wall here, and most had written funny sayings—things like: *Follow your dreams . . . but don't stalk them. Dream big, but lift with your legs, not your back. Dream on, but also give your dreams a day off now and then,* and *Sweet dreams! Or sour, or salty. Whatever you prefer.* I remembered my own quote that I'd written ages ago, which read: *If all the world's a stage . . . what about the folks behind the scenes?*

But now I saw what the Lunarian had wanted to show me: The Bad Dreams had painted over the wall during their redecorating—a horrible bright orange with drab brown paint sponged over it.

"Honestly the worst color combo I've ever seen," I said to the theatre. "How do they do it?"

I ran my hand over the paint and could still feel the indents from our carvings beneath. It was like feeling the veins on a leaf, or an old scar slightly raised from the skin. It wasn't possible to read the words any longer, but I knew them by heart, and could see them if I closed my eyes.

Well, I thought, *at least we're still here, even if I can't see us.*

Which was an interesting time to discover that I was disappearing.

Allow me to clarify: As I ran my hand over the quotes wall, I noticed that my skin wasn't looking as . . . solid as normal. Not as hand-like. Instead, it was starting to become ever-so-slightly transparent. I did the only logical thing, which was to run screaming to Circadia for help.

"AM I A GHOST NOW?!" I screamed to Circadia when I found her in the lighting department. "Do I have to haunt the theatre? Live in a graveyard? I hate grave-yards!"

"It's happening to me too," said Circadia, holding out her somewhat-sheer hand. "I suspect it's happening to all the Dreamatics."

"How are you so calm about evaporating?" I asked.

"*Because,*" she said, "I figured out the whole filter thing.

I remembered that there was this one filter up here called the Off-Kilter Filter, and it was used for those dreams that just feel . . . off. You know? Not quite right. Well, it's still here in the cupboard, but now there are TONS of them."

"Wait, really?" I asked, joining her to peer into the lighting cupboard. "They just showed up?"

"Yeah," said Circadia. "I mean, I haven't looked in here since Murph died. They must have appeared after that." She pulled out some of the filters. They were thin and sheer, of various colors, and large enough to fit over the giant spotlight.

"Chrysalism filter," I read off the first label. "Makes the dream feel like the tranquility indoors during thunderstorms. That's such a Luna word." I smiled. "So we just need to pick out the right filter for the memorable dream we're producing. And we should probably hurry since we may not, you know, exist soon."

Circadia agreed, and we shuffled through all the filters, reading the labels and trying to decide which was the perfect fit.

VELLICHOR: Makes the dream feel like the wistfulness of used bookstores.

GNOSSIENNE: Makes the dream feel like the moment of awareness that a loved one still has a private, mysterious inner life.

ANEMONIA: Makes the dream feel like a nostalgia for a time period never known.

SAUDADE: Makes the dream feel like a longing, melancholy, nostalgia for a happier time that has passed.

"Well, that's definitely a contender," said Circadia, pulling out the purple-and-blue filter and placing it to the side.

KENOPSIA: Makes the dream feel like the forlorn atmosphere of a place usually bustling with people but now abandoned and quiet, such as school hallways between classes.

DOLCE FAR NIENTE: Makes the dream feel like the pleasure of doing nothing.

UMPTY: Makes the dream feel like too much, and all in the wrong way.

HIRAETH: Makes the dream feel like homesickness for what no longer exists, a deep longing or nostalgia for a place that's now gone.

"Oh, that's the one," Circadia and I both whispered, pulling out a filter the exact color of Murph's puppy-dog eyes.

Chapter Forty-six
CHEERING FROM EVERY SEAT

When we got back to the stage with the filter, we found the Director in a screaming fight with Coco. The rest of the Dreamatics and Bad Dreams all stood to the sides. It looked like a dance-off, but I was pretty sure this didn't end in a musical number.

"We used the sign-up sheet!" yelled the Director, waving a clipboard wildly in the air. "This stage time is ours. You can't just DISREGARD the SIGN-UP SHEET!"

"WHAT SIGN-UP SHEET!?" Coco shouted back at her, his voice a forest of falling trees. "Why are you Dreamatics even still *here*? We've taken over the theatre, and we're here to stay. I don't know if you've noticed, but as you're all becoming more, shall we say, flimsy in your appearance, my own features have become much less murky, much clearer."

He was right. In all the hubbub and yelling, I had

hardly noticed that ALL the Dreamatics had taken on a sort of hazy look, the same as Circadia and me. And the Bad Dreams, especially Coco, had stopped being sort of smoky and unfocused and were now as solid as the stage we stood on. I gasped.

"But it's a sign-up sheet . . . there's an order to things . . . and it's on a clipboard with a little string and a little pencil . . ." The Director was mumbling to herself.

"Well, well, well," said Coco, towering over me. "If it isn't Casper the friendly traitor. Looking a bit ghostly these days, eh? I never should have offered you a position as a Bad Dream. You'll always just be a lowlier-than-low assistant in a soon-to-have-disappeared theatre troupe. Now get off our stage with the rest of your loser Dreamatic friends."

"Not. So. Fast," I said, putting a cloudy foot out in front of Coco. "You and I made a deal. One potion for one night without Bad Dreams. And I may be a lowlier-than-low assistant, but I've come to collect my debt."

Coco, for once, was speechless.

"One night with no nightmares for Luna," I continued. "And I choose tonight for that night. Which means you won't be needing the stage. Which means we'll be enforcing"—I grabbed the clipboard from the Director—"*the sign-up sheet.*"

I admit the last part didn't have as much intimidation as I wanted, but I was on a roll.

"So get your turnip-headed, sludgely, gormless, biffling, Mandrake-brained, flab-winked butts off our stage!"

The rest of the Dreamatics started hooting and cheering. Coco and the Bad Dreams stood with their mouths open, then begrudgingly skulked off the stage and out of the theatre.

"Now let's perform this memorable dream," I said, "before we all cease to exist forever."

"But that means . . ." said Circadia, "that you, um . . ."

"Oh right," I said, remembering what I'd perhaps been trying to forget. "I'll just go fetch the Essence of Murph and be . . . right back."

* * *

Even though I knew we were pressed for time, and even though I knew the stakes were higher than high, I didn't hurry right back to the front of the stage after fetching the Essence of Murph. I had an old friend to say farewell to, and our relationship deserved a proper goodbye.

"I saw a whale once," I said, "sitting right here."

I was sitting for the very last time in my sandcastle fort in prop storage.

"Right out that little sandcastle window. A prop whale, with water spouting out its blowhole like fireworks. It was majestic, and magical, and I think you put it there just for me."

I was talking to the Lunarian Grand, of course.

"It's so strange," I said, running my hand over the dream trinkets I'd collected through the years. "I've noticed that in the human world, you almost never know the last time you're going to see someone or do something. The last conversation, the last dance, the last dog walk on the beach. It's only the last time when you look back on it. But when you're doing it? You think, this is great, and I'm sure we'll do this so many more times. But then you don't, you know? You get too old to play with dolls, or too mature for imaginary friends, or your dog is suddenly taken away and you never get to smell his stinky breath again. And you didn't know to say goodbye. But it's not the same for me: I know this is the last time I'll be here."

I picked up a few things—the First Walk Seashell and the word *Murph* I'd collected in the Unseen Playwrights office—and put them in my pocket. Perhaps they were the magical talismans that would take our performance into the realm of the truly memorable.

Then I made my way back toward the stage, making sure to pass by all my favorite spots one last time.

"That's where we had our last snowball fight," I said to the Lunarian outside the weather closet. "And that's where the scripts would shoot down the Pipe Dream and into the Director's hands. That's where I destroyed Winks's feelings," I said, pointing to the rafters, "and that's where I cried, learning about Murph. That's where Nox taught me to plant seeds, and that's where Tuck helped me transform into a dragon. That's where Dozer dozed. And there. And there. And there . . ."

I finally made my way to the backstage and ran my hand along the velvet curtains that the Bad Dreams had torn. How many times had I stood here, in the darkness, waiting for a dream to begin?

"I know it's the last time I'll see you," I said to the Lunarian, closing my eyes, hugging the soft velvet to my face. "The last time I'll see floating dust dancing in your spotlight or feel the tingling excitement as the house-lights dim before a show. The last time I'll be by warmed by the globe lights around the stage, my personal favorite light. The last time I'll know what it feels like to be home."

I stood there, knowing I must go on into the future, but longing to stay in what was swiftly becoming my past. A place that you love is never just a place, and even after all the changes made by the Bad Dreams, there was a deeper part of the Lunarian that they could never re-model, repaint, or destroy.

"Goodbye, old friend," I whispered.

I can't say from where—there were no windows or doors or wind machines—but a warm breeze blew through the backstage area. It smelled of old leather seats and sawdust and cotton candy. An edge of the velvet curtain blew up, then curled back around my shoulders, wrapping me in its embrace.

Life is not a dress rehearsal, the Lunarian seemed to whisper straight into my heart. *The curtains are up and you are on, so get out there and give it your best shot. I'll be here watching, cheering from every seat.*

Chapter Forty-seven
FLEAS AND ALL

"So, do I just . . . drink it?"

I was standing on the stage along with all the Dreamatics. In my hand I held the bottle of Essence of Murph.

"I mean, I don't think you shampoo your hair with it," said Circadia.

"Or water flowers with it," said Nox.

"Yeah. Okay. I'll just drink it," I said.

I uncorked the bottle, the smell hitting me across the face like the tail of an overly excited dog. It smelled of puppy breath and Fritos paws and old jokes between friends. I peered into the bottle and saw that the liquid was colored with flecks of golden brown and white, the exact same as Murph's coat.

"Well, here goes nothing," I said, and put the bottle to my lips.

All the Dreamatics clutched one another as I swallowed the whole bottle in one large gulp. I didn't have time to make sense of the taste because as soon as I'd finished the potion, I began to cough. And then the coughs began to sound more like growls in the back of my throat. And then the growls became barks. I knew I was changing physically too, judging by the surprised faces of my fellow Dreamatics. I didn't really *feel* the physical changes so much—I'm a Dreamatic, after all, made to morph.

The changes I felt were *inside*. I felt . . . loyal. More loyal than I could even comprehend. And excited. Just about . . . the everything of life. I had the urge to run around in circles, and also to chase something, and also to lick someone. I couldn't see the same as before; everything had taken on tones of yellow-ish, blue-ish shades of gray. I was definitely lower to the ground, thigh-level to the other Dreamatics. And my hearing! I could hear an Anxieflea in the wall and the rain raining in the weather closet. And I had a very annoying itch on my ear, which I proceeded to scratch at with my hind claws.

I was truly a dog, fleas and all.

But the biggest change, the one that really knocked my paws off, were the smells. Oh, the smells! I smelled EVERYTHING. It was like I'd entered another world, and I couldn't stop sniffing the air.

It smelled of snow. It smelled of snow at night (which I now realized smelled very different from snow at dawn). It smelled of apples, nutmeg, gingerbread, and a hint of pine. It smelled of sweaty costumes and sawdust. It smelled of rich, warm soil after the rain, of orange peel on the tips of fingers, of the waxy sweetness of a new box of crayons. It smelled of ink and old paper and smoke in your hair after a day of camping. Of hands after they've been swinging on a metal jungle gym. Of buttons, shells, marbles, wishing pennies, and sea-worn pebbles. Of coconut puppy shampoo.

It smelled of the extra space you keep in your heart for the unimaginable. It smelled of wondrous journeys still to be taken. Of the connection felt with an author you've never met, and a glance between strangers. It smelled of freedom.

It smelled of mildew, and mothballs, and dying leaves. It smelled of ghoulies and ghosties and long-legged beasties. Of dragons and gryphons and every other untamable monster. It smelled of the green gills of the earth and of an octopus's three hearts. It smelled of pencil shavings and buttered toast, of rust and stardust, of peaches, mint, and vanilla.

The air smelled of everything.

It smelled of everything I'd known and would know.

It smelled of home.

It smelled of goodbye.

Chapter Forty-eight
A GOODBYE DUET

Here's what I know: Everyone loves a musical.

I don't love musicals, you might be saying. *In fact, I become uncomfortable watching unrealistic, overdramatic actors in deranged makeup and costumes flailing about in a synchronized cacophony.*

And I hear you. Overdramatic. Unrealistic. Synchronized. Except . . .

Well, that is . . . except . . . I still maintain: Everyone loves a musical. And if someone says they don't, that just means that the right musical for them hasn't been written yet, or performed, or reached into their heart and started it tip-tapping.

Luna fell in love with musicals the first time she saw *The Phantom of the Opera,* with all its smoke and candelabras and haunted love. And she especially loved duets.

And so, I'd decided that maybe what Luna needed to heal, and the only way she could get closure with Murph, was to have a classic form of goodbye: a duet. That was impossible in the real world, but not in our theatre of dreams and imagination.

A duet is tricky business, however.

When we'd started writing the new song in the Writers' Room, we'd used the original Nighty-Night Song lyrics for our duet. We changed the key, slowed the tempo, and gave it a try.

Goodnight
I love you
I'll see you in the morning

When it's light
And bright
And you've finished all your snoring

But no, that wouldn't work. "I'll see you in the morning" didn't have the same ring to it now that Murph was gone . . . it just sounded like a fib. A musical—especially a duet—is the time for the telling of truths. The time for the baring of emotions. The time to heal together.

And so, we had kept on writing and rewriting until we got the lyrics just right.

And now, it was the night of the big performance.

The marquee in the lobby had changed itself to read:

A GOODBYE DUET

We all gathered in a circle backstage, linking our arms and shouting the theatre's motto toward the rafters. *"Teamwork Makes the Dream Work!"*

"Hey . . . hit the hay," said Circadia, giving me a wink and heading toward the lighting booth.

Ready or not, I took my place at the side of the stage. It was time to perform our very memorable dream.

"Aaaaaand *action,*" said the Director.

As the curtains parted, the beaded eyes changed from open to closed.

And then, the spotlight slowly came up.

And then, all the world was Luna and Murph.

✳   ✳   ✳

Onstage, a dream, a memory, an imagined scene is unfolding.

Circadia has outdone herself in the lighting department—somehow managing to perfectly re-create the sunset of very late fall, right down to the lilac sky melting into yellow orange at the horizon of the ocean. It's the moment before the first snow of the year. Even the air in the theatre feels crisp and edged with the smell of sand and apples and a hint of pine.

Nox has built the set—the beach and waves and overcast sky. And on the sand there is a bed. But not just any bed; it's Luna's bed from her bedroom.

And suddenly, it's my cue: One fluffy, perfect snowflake floats down from the rafters. I burst onto the stage, leap into the air higher than I ever thought I could, and chomp that snowflake with my doggy mouth. I feel it cold on my tongue as more snow begins to fall all around like a million stars.

I wish, I wish, I wish for Luna.

And then, there she is.

Not on the stage, but the way she is in dreams—just there, all around us, in the very magic of the theatre: the way the creaking floorboards seem to speak in their own language; the way every prop, light, and velvet seat seem to know us by name; the way a stage can also be sunsets and snow, apples and stars.

I raise my nose, sniff the air, and gaze up at Luna. She leans over, just a bit, and presses her forehead to mine. She gazes into my eyes, and hers are so close that they are blurry and just about merge into one. I can't help it, and I lick her chin until she laughs. It tastes like her—like pencil shavings and peaches. Like mint and vanilla? I need another lick to really be sure.

Luna scratches behind my ear—yes, that's the spot—and when she sniffs my ear, the whole theatre whispers her voice: "Maple syrup. Your ears smell like maple syrup."

It's just a moment, this memory. It's just us, standing together, in our very first snow. Insignificant to most. How many snowflakes fall in a day? A season? A lifetime? But for me, it feels like infinite, a moment that stretches on-

ward and back, above and below, to every seat and rafter, to every corner and curtain.

 You take one snowflake.
 And you make it your own.
 And then, you have made the world.

And then, Luna and I sing our Goodbye Duet. We dance a synchronized dance, our feet as light as the wind. We each take turns with the verses and join each another on the chorus. Together, we say our sweet, soft, perfect goodbye.

Goodbye
I love you
I'll see you in my dreams

Where it's you
And me
And all is set right, or so it seems

Sweet dreams of dog parks
And eating flowers on our walks
Sweet dreams of chewing socks
Of turning back time on all the clocks

Sweet dreams of licks galore
Of being greeted at the door
Sweet dreams of belly rubs
Of mud puddles and bath-time tubs

Goodbye
I love you
I'll see you when I snore

Where we snuggle
And talk
Just like it was before

Sweet dreams of beachy walks
Of late nights and long talks
Sweet dreams of deep brown eyes
Of a dog that's patient, a dog that's wise

Sweet dreams of sunny naps
Of flying wings and treasure maps
Sweet dreams of me and you
Sweet dreams the whole night through

Goodbye
My good boy
I'll see you in my sleep

Where it's dark
And snug
And you are mine to keep

Chapter Forty-nine

I WILL ALWAYS MURPH YOU

It was morning. Luna sat straight up in bed, tears streaming down her face as she smiled a huge smile. Still in her pajamas and bare feet, she raced down the stairs, out the door, across the dewy grass, and over to her dads in the garden.

"I DREAMED OF MURPH!" she yelled.

"YOU DREAMED OF MURPH?!" yelled both her dads, throwing the weeds into the air like confetti.

"SHE DREAMED OF MURPH!" yelled all the Dreamatics, who were watching this scene unfold on the Daily Newsreel in the screening room. I barked as the others cheered and hooted and blew noisemakers like it was New Year's Eve.

"Well, what was it about?" asked Luna's dad. "Tell us *everything*."

"I thought people hated hearing about other people's dreams?" asked Luna.

"You know," said her dad Ted, "I never really understood that widely accepted notion. I love hearing about people's dreams. Wild, untamable, mysterious things. It's like a little peek into someone's weirdo soul."

"It's hard to explain . . ." said Luna. Since Murph died, she'd been having trouble talking about everything, even with her counselor and her dads. The words just seemed trapped inside some shadowy, bottom-of-a-well kind of place.

"Okay, give us the movie review version," said her dad.

This was a game they played sometimes when Luna had trouble finding the words to unravel something in life. The movie review version meant she'd just explain it like she was giving her opinion of a film, not talking about herself. And it usually worked.

"Okay, well . . ." said Luna. "I'd give this dream five out of five stars. No! Five out of five Stan the Carrots!"

"Wow," said her papa Matías, "a blockbuster."

"Do you like musicals?" continued Luna in her movie review voice. "Do you like dogs? Well, do I have a dream for you! It stars Murph the Dog and Luna the me. So don't miss this summer's greatest film: *The Goodbye Duet.* The hit single from the film will be climbing the charts: It's a remix of the Nighty-Night Song, but more beautiful and perfect."

Luna's papa wiped a tear from his eye. "I love that song."

"You're very special," said her dad Ted, hugging Luna tightly. "And so was Murph."

The dream seemed to free Luna in other ways as well: She told her dads that she was still having trouble recalling all her happy memories of Murph, but was now able to freely imagine his happy face, and that was something.

That night she even took out the stack of letters she'd written him over the years, the ones I had dream versions of in my fort. She ran her hand over the Barkday letter he would never get to read. But instead of opening it, a new letter arrived, fully formed in her imagination. A letter written to her from Murph.

Dear Luna,

Hello. It's me, Murph (the dog, in case you know anyone else named Murph).

I've never written a letter before, and usually I like to shred any paper I'm given into a million tiny pieces. I think it was my puppyhood raised on newspaper. I found the shredding very comforting, like bonsai pruning or scrapbooking.

But I digress.

You've written me so many letters—for birthdays, and Barkdays, and overnight trips, and to explain why you were mad at me for eating your school report that was written on delicious paper. So, I thought it was high time I write one back.

But what can I say?

I could tell you that I love you. That I love you more than chicken-and-liver treats and Stan the Carrot.

But that wouldn't be the truth.

The word for what I feel about you . . . I'm not even sure it's the word love. It's its own unique thing, much bigger and wider than love. I . . . I *MURPH* you.

You see, you have this whole, everything-filled life. A life of teachers, friends, and neighbors; songs, and books, and beaches; a life with your father Ted, your papa Matías, and your Lita. You have beekeeping, quote-collecting, map-making, tree research, and magic tricks. You have so much to love, and your love is beautiful and vast like pollen in the spring air, ready to make more flowers.

But my world? My heart? My everything?

Is you.

I don't have any other loves. Or friends, or teachers, or hobbies.

You are my moon, and my sun, and my planets, and the smaller moons around those planets, and every shooting star.

How lucky am I? I got to spend my whole life with you—magical, funny, wonderful you. And although I'm not able to be with you in a physical sense anymore, I want you to remember one very important thing: You could never ask for a better guardian angel than a dog, and you could never find a dog more faithful to their person than me.

Because I Murph you.

I Murph you, even if you can't see me.

I Murph you forever.

Yours, always,

Murph (the dog)

Luna had been in such darkness for so long that it was awe-inspiring to watch her imagine a letter from Murph. She seemed to hold her head a little higher, and the light in her eyes was a little brighter. It was almost as if she'd been living under a storm cloud, and the dream of Murph had finally, *finally*, let in some light.

And in through that sliver of light came an idea.

"I'm going to volunteer at the animal shelter," Luna announced to her dads that evening at dinner.

"I love that idea," said her dad Ted.

"Tell us *everything*," said her papa Matías.

And so, she did.

Chapter Fifty

CLOUDY WITH A CHANCE OF TEETH

Things at the Lunarian were looking up as well. The Dreamatics were back to their formerly solid state and no longer disappearing. I was still a dog, but a non-vanishing dog, and that was a vast improvement.

On top of that, the Worryworts, Anxiefleas, and Fretlettes seemed to have overstayed their welcome. They were being chased out of the theatre in droves by mothlike High Spirits, Happy Thoughts, Jubilations, Lily-Laughters, and fluttering Mirths and Merriments. Several Little Rays of Hope nipped at the Worryworts' heels, and soon, all the worries, anxieties, and frets were nowhere to be seen.

And then there was the marquee. The Lunarian changed it to read:

TONIGHT'S SHOW
IT'S A WONDERFUL LIFE (WITHOUT YOU)
STARRING
THE LUNARIAN GRAND

Which was interesting, since the Bad Dreams were still at the theatre, all of them skulking around like slugs, leaving their slimy stink on the place.

"Do you get the feeling like something's about to happen?" asked Circadia.

After exiting the screening room we'd all gathered near the double doors at the very back of the theatre, watching the stage and wondering what came next.

"Yeah, like that electric feeling before a thunderstorm," added Dozer.

"OH, THE SUSPENSE!" yelled Winks.

But then something *did* happen: The two gargoyle statues flanking the upper corners of the stage twisted their faces toward each other and changed their expressions to look as if they were singing a duet. They started to make a noise, a low rumbling, like a crater being moved from its place after endless years. I'd seen those statues as octopuses, owls, gryphons, foxes, and most recently these gargoyles, but I'd never seen them *move.*

"Are you catching this?" asked Rodenkirk, pointing his ratty claw toward the top of the stage.

The other Bad Dreams looked as well and watched as the two statues stood up from their hunched positions, cracked their backs, and slowly peeled their clawed feet away from the base that held them.

"That can't be good," said Tadtroll, looking to Coco for guidance.

"They're not that big," said Coco. "We can take them."

But then the statues jumped down from the top of the stage with a thundering crash, towering over all the Bad Dreams like elephants over mice.

"Forced perspective can be confusing, I guess," said Rodenkirk.

Coco thrust Rodenkirk in front of him at the gargoyles, while the rest of the Bad Dreams fled down the stairs and into the audience. But safety was not to be found there either.

"IT'S LIKE THE SURFACE OF THE SUN!" yelled Maleficara, shielding her eyes. Every spotlight in the theatre had aimed itself at the Bad Dreams, who were now huddled together in the first row, eyes shut against the blazing brightness.

Suddenly, the blinding spotlights turned off, and the Bad Dreams opened their stunned eyes to see that something was starting to rain down on them.

"What is that?!" they yelled.

"Something is falling from the sky!" yelled Coco. "OW!"

"They're . . . they're . . . TEETH," said Tadtroll.

"Not just any teeth," I said. I'd recognize those chompers anywhere—they were award-winning teeth props from Luna's dreams, made by Nox and the Dreamatics' prop department.

The other Bad Dreams all gave very high-pitched screams. Glüm proceeded to faint.

After the dental deluge, the Lunarian really got going. It opened the weather closet and unleashed everything inside all at once. Scorching heat, bolts of lightning, a small tornado, and balls of hail ricocheted off the seats and floors like icy Ping-Pong balls.

"I'm so hot!" yelled Maleficara, trying to disrobe from the darkness that shrouded her, and failing. "Now I'm freezing!" she screamed, pulling the darkness more tightly around her like a winter cloak. "WE NEED TO GET OUT OF HERE."

Not. So. Fast, the Lunarian seemed to say in reply.

From the hallways behind the stage came a sound like a stampede of wildebeests. The Bad Dreams all turned toward it, their faces screwed up in fear.

"What now?" asked Coco. "Someone should just burn this place down!"

As if in reply to his horrible suggestion, a herd like no other came around the corner: First came the Daffodragon, with its wild colors and head like a gigantic daffodil, and Winks riding on its back, cape billowing behind, conductor's baton raised high in the air like a sword.

"*Vive Le Saboteur!*" cried Winks.

"Whoa!" shouted the Director. "Where did you get that?"

"I don't remember!" said Winks in return.

They were followed by Spineyswiney cactus pigs, a gaggle of Oakofold tree-sized trolls, and one fabulous Razzmatazzacorn sneezing glitter like a fire-breathing dragon.

The group of creatures from the Department of Forgotten Things hulked toward the Bad Dreams, pushing them back until they were all forced to sit down in the front row of theatre seats, staring up at the creatures that were surely about to devour them.

"I really hate this theatre," said Coco.

Then why don't you GET OUT, the Lunarian seemed to say in reply by way of tipping back the seats the Bad Dreams were sitting in, then springing them forward as hard as possible.

"AHHHHHHHHHHH!!!" yelled the Bad Dreams as they all sailed through the air as if launched from a cannon.

I watched as they flew higher and higher past the rafters, sailing into the darkness, sailing into the nothingness, sailing into the infinite beyond or wherever bad dreams go until, on some faraway day, they find an opening to visit once again.

The Dreamatics all stood at the doors of the theatre, too shocked to move. On one door, a sign appeared, written in perfect calligraphy on white parchment. The letters were too faint to read at first, but slowly came into focus, as if the ink was given power and depth by the very act of being read.

THEATRE UNDER ORIGINAL MANAGEMENT
LOVE,
THE DREAMATICS

Chapter Fifty-one
THE DORMYS

"**D**ormir . . ." said Circadia when the regular glowing stage lights came back up and the Lunarian's revenge had ended. "How are we possibly ever going to say goodbye to you when you go into Luna's memory?"

I wagged my tail. Seeing the theatre looking and acting like its old self, seeing how happy it had made Luna and the Dreamatics, what more could I ask?

"I have an idea about that," I said. "As you all are probably aware by now, the Bad Dreams destroyed all our old Snory Awards."

"MONSTERS," said Winks. "The audacity. The nerve. THE HORROR."

"So, I thought as a little goodbye surprise," I continued, "I'd give out some awards of my own. Except I don't have any gold pillow trophies. These will just be called . . . the Dormys, I guess. Um, named after me. Lowly assistant Dormir."

"You're not just an assistant anymore," said the Director. "You're our head writer. Our lead actor. Our hero."

"The premiere of a new awards show!" said Winks. "I wish I'd worn my sequin tux. Does anyone have an extra sequin tux with them?"

"Maybe I'll stumble across one," I said. "Everyone take five while I get the Dormys ready. I'll see you all in the front row of the theatre."

*　　*　　*

"If you'll all be seated," I said when I returned.

Everyone rushed to sit down in the front row, buzzing with anticipation.

"The first Dormy of the evening," I announced, "goes to someone who *directs* us all to be our truest selves. The Boss Who Can't Be Beat Award goes to . . . the Director!"

The award was, of course, handmade in a bit of a hurry by yours truly—I'd used some glue and glitter to decorate a T-shirt with the slogan *A BOSS WHO CAN'T BE BEET* in the middle and a poorly drawn purple vegetable underneath.

The Director took the award and stared at it, a fake frown on her face. "I . . . I don't particularly like . . . puns," she said.

"Of course you don't," I said, giving her a big hug.

The other awards were mostly drawings of trophies, and went as follows: the Dormy for Weaver of Transformations to Tuck, for helping us all understand that it's not the costumes we wear, but what's inside that remains true. The Dormy for Steadfastness to Dozer, for making us all feel safe, as if we were eternally in a cozy bed on a stormy night. The Dormy for Best Encourager of Growth to Nox, the caregiver of our cast, a nurturer of night blooms, a steward of seeds. And an Honorary Dreamatic Award to Greeph, who wasn't a Dreamatic, but had been a true friend nonetheless.

"Me?" said Greeph, looking astonished as he climbed onto the stage. "I'm honored, really! Oh my. I guess I'd like to thank . . . everyone I've ever met. And sonnets. Limericks. Elegies. Ballads. Villanelles. Soliloquies. Odes . . ."

"Oh, do you hear that?" I said, giving Greeph an affectionate squeeze and ushering him offstage. "I think it's that music that plays if somebody's speech goes over the time limit."

The Dreamatics all cheered and whistled for Greeph, who beamed with pride.

"This next Dormy is a very personal one," I said, my voice catching a bit in my throat. "The Dormy for Light of Our Life . . . Light of *My* Life to Circadia. We'll be apart soon when I go into the Memory Bank, but just the thought of you will help illuminate my path."

Circadia wiped a tear, and hugged me, and accepted her award.

"That brings us to our last award of the evening," I continued. "A very special award. The Dormy for biggest heart. The kind, thoughtful, helpful, cares-about-everyone award. This one goes to the most individualistic individual. To the life of the party. To the snappiest dresser. That's right . . . the Defender of Our Theatre Dormy goes to . . . *Le Saboteur*. Also known as . . . Winks!"

"Me?" said Winks, tears filling his eyes.

After he'd walked onstage and I'd handed him his prize, I leaned in for a hug and whispered, "You know I didn't mean the stuff I said to the Bad Dreams, right? This Dormy is what I really think. What we *all* think."

"Oh, I knew," said Winks, though I wasn't quite sure. "I know now," he said, hugging me tightly. The rest of the Dreamatics joined us onstage, Winks and me at the center of a big group hug.

"I think it's about time for me to go," I said softly. "I really hope once I'm in Luna's Memory Bank as Murph that all her good memories of Murph come back."

"One last thing before you go," said Circadia, interrupting our group hug and tearful sniffling.

She turned toward me, holding Murph's collar.

"This appeared on the prop table," she said.

"I guess that's the Lunarian's way of saying it's time for me to go," I said, my voice soft with sadness.

Gently, Circadia clasped the collar around my neck.

And suddenly, with the collar on, I felt it—the very essence of being a dog that I'd never completely understood until that moment. I truly *belonged* to someone— not in the possessive ownership kind of way, but in the beautiful way, the way the things you love belong to you.

Your best friend's smile or your gramma's perfume or a certain line from a certain song. They belong to you because you love them so much that they become a part of you.

That's how I now understood I belonged to Luna.

I was a part of her. And she was a part of me. I was a memory being called home.

And my heart beat like never before: *Luna, Luna, Luna.*

Chapter Fifty-two

THE MURPHLESS MEMORY GARDEN

And so, alone this time, I made my way down the trap-door elevator, along Memory Lane (which was now Broadway musical themed), and to the Memory Bank.

"So, how exactly will this work?" I asked Bloomwit the owl, the Memory Vault Keeper on duty.

"Unclear," said Bloomwit. "Memories are different for everyone. I've read one can be organized like a supermarket, or into a puzzle box, or even endless filing cabinets with folders of memories."

"What's it like in Luna's Memory?"

Bloomwit shook her head. "We vault keepers aren't allowed inside; only the memories go in there. But since you Dreamatics made a memorable dream starring you as Murph, you're technically a memory now, and should be allowed inside."

"Well, what should I do?" I asked.

"Sit," said Bloomwit. "Or maybe lie down. Definitely stay."

And so, like a good dog, I sat. And waited. And stayed.

And, to my shock, once Bloomwit had flown away, a door appeared. Well, a doggy door, to be exact, right in the wall of the Memory Bank.

"I guess Luna's Memory is waiting for me . . ."

So long, Wormwood and Bloomwit.

So long, Lunarian Grand.

So long, Dreamatics.

So long, Dormir.

I walked through the doggy door, leaving behind my old life, and moving forward to give Luna back her memories. The plastic flap tapped me on the behind as it closed, and when I looked back, it had already disappeared.

I gazed around and was relieved: not a filing cabinet in sight. No supermarkets or puzzles. I suppose I should have known that Luna's Memory would be something unique, something special.

I should have guessed she'd have a Memory that looked like a secret garden.

Every inch and corner of the garden—which seemed to stretch on forever—was covered with trees, bushes, and flowers. But these weren't like any flora I'd ever seen in Luna's world.

Does that bush have . . . coconut date bars growing on it, I wondered.

I investigated, and sure enough there was a bush that looked like any other, but instead of berries it was growing entire coconut date bars, just like Lita made for Luna.

There were trees growing maps for leaves, and trees with tiny orbs hanging among their branches like planets; there were bushes blooming with seashells, sand dollars, and starfish; there were flowers with petals made of Luna's favorite quotes, and lines from favorite movies.

There was, however, one tree that was different from the rest. While the other trees seemed to be mostly in bloom, one tree was dormant—the tree was large, and fur covered, but barren of leaves or flowers.

This must be the Murph Tree, I thought, sniffing closer. Wind howled through the empty branches as if the tree stood in its own personal winter. Upon closer inspection I saw that there was one blossom, small and shaped like a snowflake. *The duet,* I thought. *It's a start, I suppose.*

I wasn't sure how a Memory Garden worked exactly, so I just tried sniffing at the blooms on an adjacent bush. The flower was shaped like a tennis ball, and so I thought, *Maybe this is a Murph memory as well?* As I sniffed, a mist of pollen rose out of the flower, expanding into the air around me. It started to take the form of figures and objects, spilling into the garden and fitting in the best it could. It felt as if two moments in time had overlapped. The air in the forest had been daytime but was now covered in areas of murky sunset. Between the plants and vines, there was an oven, a kitchen table, and a cuckoo clock on a wall. Above me, the kitchen lights were now nestled in the branches of a tree.

Around the corner came Luna's dad

"I bought some new tennis balls," said Ted, his voice sounding like an echo of an echo. He thumped the tennis ball off the floor, once, twice, three times.

Cue Murph! I thought excitedly. I remembered this moment, and I knew that when he heard the ball, Murph came racing into the kitchen and crashed into the table. Everything was fine, except maybe Murph's pride.

But to my surprise, Murph didn't appear. Instead, Luna helped her dad set the table, putting out silverware and napkins like nothing was amiss. After that, the pollen mist dissipated, and the ghost-like memory faded away. I was left in the Memory Garden once more.

I tried again. I found a bush abloom with summer memories—lemonade blossoms, beach ball berries, and flowers shooting sparks. I sniffed a sparkler, careful not to singe my nose. Around me in the garden appeared a ghostly vision of a family picnic, complete with a fire and s'mores. And I knew—*I knew*—that every time that Luna roasted a marshmallow, she would share it with Murph. And they would both get sticky, and laugh, and I would think, *Who needs unsticky whiskers or hands in a world as wonderful as this?*

But this time Luna ate her marshmallow alone and there was not a Murph in sight.

Finally, I tried sniffing one last memory in a patch of

flowers that looked and smelled like pancakes dripping with butter and syrup. I watched as Lita appeared in front of her stove flipping pancakes. She flipped several successfully, but one flopped instead of flipped, and landed on the floor. In real life I knew that Murph had run over and gobbled up the pancake and everyone had laughed. But in this new scene they all just stared at the pancake, shrugged, and went back to eating.

"I just thought . . ." I said to the ghost family now fading away. "I thought once I was here, the memories of Murph would come back."

I don't know what I'd expected would happen when I entered the garden. A marching band of Murphs? A parade of dog floats? To be greeted by a team worth of Murphs and hoisted on their shoulders like we'd just won the big game?

Maybe not.

But I hadn't expected *this.*

This under-pancaking of pups.

This drought of dogs.

This Murphless Memory Garden.

Chapter Fifty-three
WAFFLES!

Though the memories in the garden remained Murph-less, I was still able to watch news about Luna via new memories that grew in the garden. Any morsel of Luna's life interested me, as always, and even more so now that I was starved for company. They made me feel connected, part of the everything; they made me wish the inhabitants would come spend their time with me in the garden.

One day, while making my rounds, I noticed one of these new memory blooms. It was a shivering flower, small and scared.

"Now, what have we here?" I asked.

I sniffed the memory, getting top notes of wood chip with some mellow smells of newspaper and cat food.

When the memory unfolded around me in the garden, there was Luna, sitting at a long table in a brightly painted room. The sign on the wall read: *MSPCA Animal Shelter, New Volunteer Day. Welcome!*

"Let's all share what brought us here," said the orientation leader.

"I'm here because I love animals but my sons are allergic," said a woman.

"I'm here because my college requires us to volunteer," said a teenage boy, "and, um, I have a cat who I miss back home."

"I'm retired," said an older man. "I was in the navy, and then opened a pet grooming business with my wife. She's gone now, but I think I still have the skills to fancy up some of these animals and get them adopted."

Finally, it was Luna's turn. Since it was her memory, I could hear the thoughts running through her head in a whisper: *I'm here because my therapist said the final stage of trauma therapy is to integrate the loss into myself, and this is what I came up with. I'm here because everyone keeps telling me grief takes time, so I need a way to pass time. I'm here because I'm too sad to be around humans.*

But what she said aloud was: "I'm here because I had a dog. And now I don't. I'm not ready for another dog but maybe I'm ready to . . . be around dogness in general."

"Would you like to share a favorite memory of your dog?" asked the orientation leader. "Sometimes sharing happy memories can help."

I gulped.

Luna gulped.

"Um . . . no thanks," said Luna. "My good memories of

my dog are sort of . . . dormant right now. Hibernating. Asleep."

The other volunteers nodded with understanding. I whined with worry.

As time moved on, more memories came from Luna's volunteer time at the shelter. Each time one arrived, it was planted by the bees in the same spot, and soon that bush was covered in blooms.

I sniffed and sniffed and watched it all unfold around me in ghostly magic.

The volunteer coordinator noted that Luna had a way with words and creativity, so she put Luna in charge of naming animals that came in without names. One week she gave all the animals book-related names: Matilda, Narnia, Ramona, and Eloise. The next week, all food names: Gordita, Meringue, Wonton, Rhubarb, Mooncake, and Baguette. Finally, the week after she gave all the animals pun names (Mary Puppins, Chew-barka, Salvador Dogi, and Orville Redenbarker), the volunteer coordinator rotated her to a position with slightly *less* creativity, but even more dogness: animal socialization.

The next animal shelter memory showed Luna sitting beside a metal cage that contained the tiniest, saddest, most frightened looking dog maybe in all the world. The tag on his door read:

Waffles!

"So . . . Waffles," said Luna. "You're new here, huh?" She paused, clearly searching for conversation. "How about the smells in this place? Well, you probably like it; you're a dog. Kinda smells like . . . wet fur and hay."

Waffles lifted his head and sniffed the air, then furrowed his eyebrows in a worried expression, his tail wrapping around his body like a shield.

"I like your coat," said Luna. "Reminds me of a painted pony. Do you know what they are? They're really beautiful. Just like you will be once you've had a bath."

The dog looked a tad insulted.

"Or even without the bath," said Luna.

After a bit more one-sided conversation it was time for Luna to go. She knew enough not to try and pet Waffles, but she did kneel at his gate and say this:

"I had a dog," she said, "and I miss him terribly. I know what it's like to be scared and sad—so sad that you can't even remember the best memories of your best friend. I hope *you* have some good memories to keep you warm. And I hope you have sweet dreams. I hope you dream about whatever you love most, Waffles."

Chapter Fifty-four

DANCING HAM SANDWICHES IN SLICED PICKLE HATS

The animal shelter memory with Waffles faded away, and I was once again alone in the Memory Garden.

I sighed, rolling onto my back and closing my eyes. I tried to imagine the theatre and what was going on there right now. It would be after rehearsals, but before the nightly show, the fresh smell of newly grown sets filling the air.

"Where are the dancing ham sandwiches?!" yelled the Director in my imagination. "They're supposed to be wearing little sliced pickle hats, not globs of mustard that look like bad blond wigs!"

"Sorry, boss," said Tuck. "Costume department is on it."

I smiled when I saw what the Director was wearing: a shirt with a purple beet drawn on it and the words *A BOSS THAT CAN'T BE BEET* across the front.

I guess she must have liked it after all, I thought. *Or maybe it's laundry day.*

"Is this unflattering and hopeless enough?" yelled a voice from the rafters. It was Circadia, hanging up a light that was shaped like a school lunch tray and giving off the fluorescent brightness found in school cafeterias.

"It's not quite bleak enough," said the Director. "Could you make one bulb flicker?"

The others buzzed around the theatre as well. Winks waved his baton while conducting the "Eating Lunch at 10:15 a.m. Overture" with his orchestra. Dozer nodded off putting the dream title on the marquee.

Thinking about all of them, my heart started to ache, just a bit. I missed my Dreamatics, and wished I could talk to them. But that was impossible. Now they existed only in my imagination.

In my daydream, the scene onstage changed, and the set was a garden much like the one in Luna's memory. There were tall trees reaching to the rafters, and their roots spread downstage and into the audience. All the Dreamatics stood around, waiting.

"I said ACTION!" yelled the Director.

I stood in the center of the stage, dumbfounded. Everyone, including the Director, was staring expectantly at me.

"Um, line?" I asked. Perhaps someone was on book. "Line . . . please?"

But in return, there was only silence.

"What's my line?" I asked, panicking. "Is it woof? Arf? Growl? What do I do?"

You know what to do, the Lunarian seemed to say. *You know because you're a Dreamatic. So step into that spotlight and . . .*

My eyes snapped open. The daydream faded, and I was back in the real Memory Garden. Back to being alone and confused.

Am I still a Dreamatic? I wondered.

Or a memory?

Neither? Both?

Perhaps, given my personality, I was Luna's pain. Her shame. Her lowlier-than-low moments of low self-esteem.

No, I thought. *I'm not those things, not anymore.*

I had changed during my journey. I'd ventured into the unknown, become a Bad Dream, written a memory, and said goodbye to all I'd ever known.

I was . . . her bravery.

I was her never-give-up. Her keep-going-no-matter-what. I had been totally afraid, and I had totally done it all anyway. I was the part of Luna that was capable of anything.

I thought about the trees onstage, and the roots. I recalled Luna's tree phase, when she learned how trees couldn't speak, but could send signals to one another through their roots. Maybe that's what my daydream had been—the connection I still had with the Lunarian and other Dreamatics, trying to tell me what to do.

So step into that spotlight and . . . act?

I decided it was worth a try.

And so, in the Memory Garden, I got up from my daydreaming spot and I sniffed a flower I knew contained a missing Murph memory, and when the dust rose around me, instead of just watching, I *acted*. It was a memory of Luna walked along, feeding the ducks in the park. I knew that Murph had been there with her, so I played his role, and chased after the ducks. And wouldn't you know it? The ducks *ran*. They dove into the lake. They squawked and flapped all because of me.

I ran around the Memory Garden, sniffing and playing Murph in every memory I could recall.

I acted as Murph watching Luna on a carousel.

I played the part of Murph seeing a whale diving into the air on a summer day long past. It breeched out of the Memory Garden, waves splashing around it capped with white.

We found a four-leaf clover, put it with the others in a tiny plastic treasure chest.

I sat beside Luna and watched a planetarium on her bedroom ceiling while around me in the garden appeared planets like ringed Jupiter, supernovas frozen mid-explosion, and a Milky Way full of stars.

I sat, panting and exhausted from starring in so many

memories, when I noticed that something had changed on the Murph tree.

Are those . . . buds? I wondered, walking over to investigate.

Sure enough, flower buds had appeared on every branch of the Murph tree. They were closed, but I had a feeling, like all things, they would open in their own time. Nothing blooms all year, after all. Nature had patience, and so would I—with the memories, with myself, and with Luna.

I would take my time and repopulate every last memory with Murph.

But would it be enough?

Would it bring the real memory Murph back for good?

Chapter Fifty-five

HALF AN INCH EACH DAY

While I acted as Murph in Luna's memories, I was also hopeful—hopeful for another update about Luna and Waffles. Luckily, new memories steadily arrived, and I was able to watch . . .

Waffles inching closer to Luna, just half an inch each day.

Luna trying to give Waffles a ball. Waffles cowering, and rolling over to play dead.

Luna trying to give Waffles a treat. Waffles ignoring the treat. Could be a trap.

Luna taking Stan the Carrot out of her bag and placing it on the lawn between her and Waffles. Stan basking in the sunshine. Waffles shivering with nerves.

Waffles inching closer to Luna, just half an inch each day.

Waffles watching bugs, and lying in the grass, and eating crunchy leaves.

Luna giving Waffles a treat. Waffles taking the treat, but not actually eating it.

Waffles resting his head on Stan the Carrot. Waffles closing his eyes. Waffles basking, for a moment, in the sunshine.

Waffles inching closer to Luna, just half an inch each day.

Waffles inching so close to Luna that he is right beside her.

Waffles inching so close that his head is on Luna's lap.

Luna letting Waffles sniff her hand, then laying it softly on his head. Waffles gazing up at her with a mix of awe and fondness.

The volunteer coordinator telling Luna that Waffles might be ready to be put up for adoption. Ready to pack his bags and leave the shelter.

Luna giving Waffles a treat, Waffles taking the treat and eating it. Luna giving Waffles another treat. Waffles taking it, digging in some leaves, and burying the treat.

"For tomorrow?" asks Luna.

For tomorrow, nods Waffles, trusting that of course she'd be there again tomorrow.

Chapter Fifty-six

BOWL, LEASH, COLLAR, BOY

Waffles was ready.

He'd trained for this. He'd given it everything his little heart had to give. And now it was finally the big day: the day he was going to meet people looking to adopt a dog.

But day after day, people would arrive, glance at him, and move along. Nobody seemed to want what Waffles could provide.

"He's too timid," they said.

"Too old."

"Too young."

"He looks like a rat that was splattered with paint."

"The thing about being different," Luna explained to Waffles, "is it's an automatic test for anyone you meet. If they treat you badly, or judge you, then you know all you need to know about them. They aren't for you. Also, as a note, rats are highly intelligent, have great memories, and contrary to popular belief they hate getting dirty."

One afternoon just as Luna was packing up her books after reading to Waffles and some of the other dogs, a boy came into the shelter. He was a little younger than Luna, small for his age, with wild hair and blue-rimmed glasses. The pregnant woman he'd come in with carefully lowered herself into a chair with a sigh, and smiled at the boy.

"Go on, buddy," she said, "tell them what you're looking for."

Luna greeted the boy. "What can I help you with? Cat? Rabbit? Dog?"

The boy stared, his eyes wide behind his glasses. He looked like he might start hyperventilating at any moment.

"What's your name?" tried Luna again. "I'm Luna, a volunteer here. I can show you some animals, and if you want to adopt one, we can get the adoption coordinator."

"I'm, um . . . dog," said the boy. "No, sorry, I'm Gary, and I'd like to meet some dogs."

"Great," said Luna, grabbing one of the forms they used to match humans and dogs. "Just a few questions. First, have you ever had a dog before?"

"No," said Gary. "Well, do imaginary dogs count?"

"I think there's a separate section for that," said Luna. Gary nodded earnestly.

"What kind of dog are you looking for?" continued Luna. "Any special size or breed?"

"Not really," said Gary. "I guess I'd like a dog who can

sleep in bed without pushing me out of it, but not one so small that I'd lose it around the house."

"Noted," said Luna. "And lastly, any temperament you'd prefer? As in, personality. Do you want an energetic dog, or a mostly lazy one? One that's super intelligent, or just regular-dog smart? A dog that likes to be social, or a dog that likes to kind of hang with you mostly?"

"I guess . . ." said Gary, "I'd prefer a dog like me."

"Meaning . . . ?" said Luna.

"I don't really have a lot of friends," said Gary. "I've been told I'm shy. And quiet. And a bit cautious. I mostly just like watching bugs and lying in the grass and stepping on crunchy leaves, stuff like that."

"Well then," said Luna, smiling a megawatt smile, "have I got a guy for you. Follow me!"

Gary followed Luna to the kennels and watched as she hooked a harness on Waffles. Waffles kept stealing glances back at the boy, feeling more curious than afraid for the first time in a long time.

"Gary, meet Waffles. Waffles, meet Gary," said Luna.

"What a terrific name," said Gary.

Gary put out his closed hand to Waffles to let him sniff it. And then, slowly, put his palm on the dog's head, and Waffles closed his eyes. The boy was small. And shy. And sweet. Waffles's life before the shelter had been very bad, but it had made him very good at reading humans.

Luna busied herself around the yard, picking up toys

and sticks, letting Gary and Waffles get to know each other. Within a few minutes of Gary sitting cross-legged on the grass, Waffles had curled up on the boy's lap.

"Oh, wow," said Gary, grinning from ear to ear.

Luna could see the boy was already falling in love. She knew because she'd looked at a dog that way once too.

"Now he's licking my face," squealed Gary, falling onto his back in a fit of dog kisses.

Luna laughed. And in that moment, watching the pair, she knew this: Maybe she wasn't quite ready for a new dog, but someday she would be. She could feel it. Waffles had trusted her, and in turn, she had started to trust herself again. Her heart was on its way.

*　　*　　*

A few days later, after Gary's mom met with the adoption coordinator and the shelter performed a home visit, it was finally the day of Waffles's adoption. Gary arrived wearing a collared shirt and clip-on tie for the occasion. Waffles had been washed and groomed, care of Luna, and smelled like coconut puppy shampoo.

As the adults finished the last of the paperwork by the desk, Luna went to say her goodbyes. Gary sat nearby, giving them a moment together. Waffles shook slightly with excited nerves, and Luna sat in front of him, petting him until he'd calmed a bit.

"So, big day," she said. "I really am going to miss you."

You're telling me, kid, Waffles seemed to say with his eyes.

"I got you a few going home presents," she continued, unzipping her backpack.

Waffles tilted his head to one side, then the other. *Presents? What is this word presents?*

From her bag Luna pulled out a dog bowl, a collar, and a leash. Lastly, she pulled out Stan the Carrot.

"These belonged to my dog, Murph," said Luna. "I've held on to them for a while now. But I want them to have another life. With you. I want you to have them."

Waffles's eyes grew wide. *For . . . me?* he seemed to say.

He sniffed the bowls, the leash, the collar. Luna's dads had helped her get a new dog tag made at the pet shop, and on it was the name WAFFLES engraved along with Gary's phone number and address.

Waffles had never owned anything, not one single thing to call his own. And now, he did.

A bowl

A leash.

A collar.

And a boy.

Waffles picked up Stan the Carrot, gently, and looked at Luna one last time. He then trotted over to Gary, laying the carrot on his boy's lap. *I am not a rich dog,* he seemed to say. *I don't have much. This is one of my only possessions, but I'd like you to have it, just the same.*

Chapter Fifty-seven
FULL BLOOM

By the time the Waffles's memory disappeared, my cheeks were wet, and my throat was tight. I wasn't completely sure why these new memories were making me so emotional, but I felt it had something to do with my wish for Luna to be back to her old self, and the realization that she would *never* be her old self again. And that maybe that wasn't a bad thing.

Luna had gone through a horrible trauma. She'd had something happen that she could hardly stand the thought of. But she had worked on it, and moved closer to her pain, just half an inch each day. She found a way to talk about it, she slowly trusted, she felt her way through it. And on the other side, Luna was . . . different.

I'd never seen her do volunteer work like this before or be so careful and gentle and patient. It meant that Luna had the power now to help Waffles heal—a power she didn't have before she lost Murph. I'd been wishing that Luna would be carefree again, careless, but the truth was in front of me: Luna had taken her trauma and mixed it with all the good and light inside her, and it had become another part of her. The part of her that was able to see herself in Waffles, and help Waffles see his own hurt in her. Luna had absorbed the loss and let it carve her like sand into a different, kinder, more understanding person.

I knew then that the pain she felt would never completely disappear. But there would be intermissions, longer and longer ones as more time passed. And during those breaks in the darkness, there would be Friday-flavored days. There would be the fondness of new dogs, the crunch of leaves, the warmth of the sun, and the hum of everything—*everything*—in between.

After I saw Waffles find his forever home, my heart felt full of nostalgia. I sniffed at the Goodbye Duet memory, the one we'd created in the Lunarian. It unfolded like fog around me. The phantom snow fell in the bright and sunny garden, and there I came, leaping through the snow to catch a flake in my doggy mouth.

Except it *wasn't me.*

This dog had a natural dog-like grace that I'd never quite gotten the hang of after living my whole life on two legs. A twinkle in his eyes. A certain something in his smile.

This dog . . . this dog was *Murph.*

The real Murph.

And that's when I saw that the Murph tree had changed

as well. Where there had once been bare branches, then buds, there were now colorful flowers in the shape of dog toys and treats, of memories and moments.

The tree, like Luna's heart, had finally started to bloom.

Chapter Fifty-eight
A COLLECTION OF KEYHOLES

Murph!
    Murph?!
MURPH!

The real Murph had returned to all Luna's memories. (I knew because I checked them all.) He was back chasing tennis balls and eating pancakes off the floor, back making snow angels, dozing in the sun, stargazing, and everything in between.

"Welcome back, memory Murph," I said. "You have been very, very, *very* much missed."

As I sniffed around all the Murph memories, my nose and eyes were so focused on the ground that when I bumped into the door, I didn't even notice at first.

"Ow," I said, shaking my head. "I can't believe I walked right into the door."

I continued sniffing until I realized what I'd just said.

"WHAT DOOR?" I yelled, spinning around.

But sure enough, there in the base of the Murph tree, I could see the edge of a small door partly covered in ivy. The door was wooden and under the doorknob there was a keyhole shaped like a crescent moon. I moved closer, putting one eye to the moon and trying to see what was on the other side.

"Ack!" I yelled, jumping back.

The door had moved. It had done a little shimmy, as if it was tickled by my whiskers when I'd tried to peer through the keyhole. I laughed, and the wood seemed to shiver with laughter as well. The door knocker above my head banged *thump, thump, thump* like a metal heart.

And then, the keyhole changed shape.

It changed from a crescent moon to a seashell, just like the ones Luna and Murph used to collect on the beach. I watched, mesmerized, as it morphed into a collection of keyholes as if it couldn't quite decide what sort of key would open it—one moment it was a snowflake, the next it was in the shape of a bumblebee. The keyhole became a potion bottle, a pencil, a castle, a teakettle, a bat, and a lantern.

The Lunarian had many doorways, of all shapes and sizes. But there were other doors too, I realized, ones that weren't visible to the naked eye. Love was a kind of doorway. Pain could be a doorway too. I'd learned that by watching Luna. Some doorways a person can't find on their own, located through mud, and vines, and cold, and dark. And when those doors open it's often a new version of yourself on the other side. There are doorways that lead you back to you.

I was about to share these deep thoughts with my new friend Door, when I saw that the keyhole had changed to the shape of a dog. And that dog was *glowing*.

"There's light coming through your keyhole!"

The door thumped its door knocker in surprise.

I approached, feeling like I knew that light, had seen it before.

"I think . . ." I said, "I think this was once my favorite kind of light."

I put my eye to the keyhole and looked through, then jumped away. "There's an *actual eye* looking back!"

I approached once more and looked through the keyhole. This time I realized that the eye didn't seem like a person's eye, or an animal's eye. This eye shimmered. This eye was bejeweled. This eye glittered when it caught the light.

And then, as it had done many times before, the beaded eye on the other side of the door gave me an unmistakable, undeniable velvet curtain *wink*.

Chapter Fifty-nine
A VERY MEMORABLE DOG

The door creaked open and just as I was gathering all my courage to walk through, a new bloom sprung to life, right above me on the Murph tree. I couldn't resist; I sniffed it, and watched the scene unfold.

Luna ran downstairs, heart pounding, and found her parents in the kitchen.

"I REMEMBER!" she cried.

"You remember what?" asked Matías. "To do your chores?"

"To clean your room?" asked Ted, smiling. "To fold your laundry?"

"I remember Murph!" she said. "I remember *everything*. Every moment, every memory, it's all back. I remember singing in the bath, and his fear of stairs, his daily rounds in the yard, and the time he sprained his tail from wagging it too much. I remember how he'd herd us to bed at night, and the way it felt to bury my head in his fur. I remember sleeping and waking together. I remember *us*. I remember *him*."

"Of course you do," said Ted. "He was a very memorable dog."

"Your heart just needed time," said Matías. "But those memories were always in there. He's a part of you, forever and always. And nothing can take that away."

Luna cried, and hugged her dads.

She smiled with joy, and pain, and thankfulness, and everything in between.

Chapter Sixty

THAT KIND OF GLOW

Once upon a dream, there was a dog.

And a door.

And a decision to be made.

The light shined through the dog-shaped keyhole—the light I now knew came from the Lunarian Grand. The door creaked toward me. It seemed to be saying, *I'm a door, silly, you know what to do.*

And so, I did.

I used my paw and swung the door wide open.

I stuck my nose around the corner. I sniffed.

I know this place, I thought. *I know this smell. Sawdust. And popcorn. And the sweet sweat of old costumes.*

It smelled . . . like home.

Behind me, I could feel the warm sun and breezes of the Memory Garden, hear the buzz of bees, smell the color green. In front of me, the sound of the ocean.

I heard a click behind me and turned to see that the door had not only closed, but had also disappeared. There was no direction but forward, so I ventured into the sandcastle. *My old fort,* I thought, except it had changed shape as well, and was now a doghouse, complete with bed, bowls, and toys. I smiled. *The Lunarian knew I was coming home.*

I tried to take my usual route to the theatre, but ended up in a new hallway, one line with candles and sconces, and in between were framed playbills. They all depicted dreams with Murph. Some of them looked new and crisp. Others were faded to various degrees, and felt more like seeing an old friend who, though aged, was still recognizable.

And at the end of the hallway, there was a large lobby. As I stepped inside, my eyes were drawn up to the lights of the marquee. It read:

DREAM A LITTLE DREAM OF MURPH
STARRING MURPH THE DOG
WORLD PREMIERE TONIGHT!

I smiled. "Now *that* sounds like a must-see show."

"Yes, even *I* couldn't nap through this one," said a voice.

It was Dozer, on a ladder, putting the finishing touches on the sign. I nodded to him, and he nodded back with a twinkle in his eyes. I sniffed my way to the door of the theatre, led by the tingling excitement of the moment when the houselights would dim, the eyes on the velvet curtains would close, and Luna's dreams would begin.

I nosed the door open and slipped inside the theatre, and something inside me leapt like a grasshopper in long grass. Before me wasn't just the most majestic, magical theatre in the universe.

Even more magical, even more beautiful, was that everyone was there.

Smiling. Waiting.

But for what?

All along the aisle leading to the stage stood the forty members of the Forty Winks Orchestra, playing a song that made me feel the exact opposite of lowlier-than-low.

At the end of the aisle, baton in hand, stood Winks.

"How does this song make you feel?" he asked.

"Like I'm dancing in the snow," I replied. "But I'm also the air, and the light, and the thrill felt by the falling snowflakes."

"PERFECTION!" he shouted dramatically. "MY HEART IS COVERED IN SEQUINS!"

I trotted to the stairs at the side of the stage, where I was met by Greeph, who was wearing a pair of paint-splattered overalls just like the ones I used to wear when I was an assistant. He held my old toolbox and was fixing a creaky board.

"Greeph!" I cried. "Are you . . . ?"

"An *official* Dreamatic!" said Greeph, a look of joy

on his face. "They even let me keep this thing as a pet."

From the front pocket of Greeph's overalls, a furry, multicolored Worrywort poked its head out, sniffing around like it wanted a treat. As I stroked its fur, I thought about the critter living full-time in the Lunarian Grand. *I guess,* I thought, *after going through something like what Luna went through, some worry and grief would always stick around. But it could integrate, make friends, and become a part of her.*

I made my way up the stairs to the stage, where I saw a perfect replica set of Luna's house—her bedroom where she'd slept with Murph, the kitchen where they'd eaten together, and even the yard where they would play and laugh and lounge in the sun.

"Welcome home," said Nox, motioning to the set she'd grown.

Real sunlight seemed to stream in through the windows of the house set, small specks of dust dancing in the gentle glow. Only one person could achieve such perfection, and I admit I couldn't contain myself when I saw her, leaping up and placing two paws on her chest, licking her cheek with a slobbery kiss.

"Good to see you too," said Circadia, laughing, hugging me right back. "Your breath is . . . interesting. I would if I could capture it in some sort of lighting . . ."

"It's him," I heard a voice say behind me. "It's you."

I watched the Director approach from the wings of the

stage. Her T-shirt had a picture of a zombie on the front and the words *CREEP CALM.*

I chuckled—some things never change. Some things I'd never *want* to have change.

"I was just about to hold auditions," said the Director. "We all gathered after we saw the marquee and a new script with that title arrived from the Unseen Playwright. I wasn't sure if a Dreamatic would finally have the ability to transform into Murph, or if someone new was going to show up and join us. I guess I was right about both."

"The Unseen Playwright is *back*?" I asked.

"As far as we can tell," said the Director. "I mean, they're still unseen, but the scripts are back to normal, and tonight's includes Murph."

"Well, won't Reverie just play the part?"

"HA!" said the Director. "Reverie ran off with the Bad Dreams when they got kicked out by the Lunarian."

"So, you're holding auditions for the dream role of Murph?" I asked.

My thoughts sailed back to my days as an assistant, standing backstage, knowing every line by heart and whispering them under my breath, loving every moment, but telling myself,

You will never be in the spotlight, Dormir.

You will never bask in that kind of glow.

You will never capture moments, stir hearts, feel the thrill of the first or last act.

You will always be only what you are: a lowly stage-hand, a set painter, an assistant to all but never the star.

Still, I had thought. *Still.*

Even a dream like me is allowed to dream.

"Um . . . do you think . . ." I asked, "Do you think I could audition?"

"Oh, I don't think you need to audition for this role," said the Director. "I think you already got the part."

She turned to the other Dreamatics, who by now had gathered around us, some wiping tears from their eyes.

"You all really do put the *dramatic* in *Dreamatics,*" I said.

They all laughed and held hands, leaning against one another for support.

"I'd like you all to welcome our new actor, thespian, *star,*" said the Director. "Welcome back, Dormir."

Everyone clapped and chatted with excitement.

"Circadia?" called the Director.

Somewhere in the darkness, Circadia did her magic and flipped a switch, and suddenly, I was bathed in spotlight.

I turned my face to the light. It warmed not just my fur, but also a place deep inside me that now fully understood what I'd always longed for. It wasn't stardom or applause. It was this: a family, a purpose, a dream come true.

Welcome home, Murph, I thought.

Welcome to the show.

Welcome . . . to the Lunarian Grand.

EPILOGUE

O nstage, a dream is unfolding.

Or is it a memory? Something imagined? Something made of all these things, and dappled, like light through tree leaves, with nostalgia and wonder?

"Ah, the eternal question," says Luna's dad, played in the dream by one of the Dreamatic actors.

"But I suppose the most important part of a dream," he continues, "is the mystery, the one beyond reach or reason or language. A dream takes a while to rise in the morning, especially when it has not had its breakfast."

Luna, the dreamer, gives an eye roll to her dad, realizing that perhaps she needs a more neutral source for this information. She gets down under the table and lies flat on the floor on her stomach until she is nose to nose with Murph.

The dog wags his tail with joy.

"So, what do you dream about?" asks Luna.

Murph, in reply, licks Luna's nose.

Luna places her hands on each side of Murph's face. "Just tell me. I won't tell anyone. I promise."

"Okay, fine," says Murph. "I'll tell you. But you must pinkie swear to keep it your secret."

"Of course," says Luna, looping her pinkie under Murph's paw.

"First, I'll tell you what I don't dream about," says Murph. "I don't dream about Stan the Carrot. I love him, but he has never appeared in a dream. I don't dream about squirrels. Or the evil dishwasher. Or smells at the beach. Or watermelon, sprinklers, delivery people. My dreams are not made of cheese, or plums, or unwound fingerprints. They do not fly like a lost kite string, or follow me all day purring at the windows, or hang like a spider's web full of dew. They are not like a music box's last note, or an old firefly, blinking its last light."

"Thank you for clarifying," says Luna, smiling. "So then what do you dream about?"

"When I dream," says Murph, "I dream of your face. And of licking your face. Your face tastes like sunlight and ice cream. I dream of playing fetch with you, and watching TV with you, and waiting for you to come home from school. I dream of swimming with you, of running through the long grass with you, of nibbling on the edges of whatever paper you happen to be holding. I even dream of sleeping beside you, which is like dreaming of dreaming, I suppose."

Luna's heart, even if only in a dream, feels like it might burst. She strokes Murph's head, rubs his ears the way he likes. The old dog gives a pleased sigh and closes his eyes.

"Perhaps," he says, "yes, perhaps I'll go dream of you now."

A BRIEF EXPLANATION OF THE EPILOGUE

Luna awakens from the dream, visions of herself as a young girl with Murph fading, slowly, the way dreams do in the morning light. She wipes a hand over her wrinkled face and feels wet tears. They are not, she knows, tears of sadness, but rather from a full heart overflowing with joy.

For you see, throughout her whole life, some nights (not every night, but some nights), Luna dreams of Murph.

She dreams of him as a teenager.

And a young adult.

And even when she is a very old woman, tucked up warm in her bed.

She closes her eyes, falls into sleep, and there he is, Murph, young again and running toward her at full speed.

These are Luna's favorite dreams, the nights she looks forward to the most: when she's reunited, briefly, with her very best friend.

Sometimes in her dreams, Murph is a puppy again, full of energy, teething and destroying everything he can get his paws on.

Sometimes he is a very old dog, old in a way he never got to be in Luna's world. He has patches of white fur around his eyes and nose. In these dreams, she sits beside him quietly, one arm draped over his back, and they both turn their faces toward the warm sun.

But most of the time, Murph is just Murph. With his one crooked whisker and stinky breath and deep brown eyes. Together, they eat watermelon, run through the sprinkler. They catch snowflakes and sing duets during baths. They play and romp, whisper and cuddle, they lie in the grass or leaves or snow, happy to be together, even if just for one more night.

In dreams, Murph is still full of lightness.

And kindness.

And everything, everything good.

I'll tell you a secret, though: Those nights aren't just Luna's favorites; they're my favorites as well. Not because I get to be Dormir-the-Actor, a star in the spotlight, but because I no longer have to wonder what it would be like to be tucked in at night, to love and be loved in return. By helping Luna, I somehow helped myself too. I am a dream come into myself. I am a dream come true. I know, finally, what it feels like to bask in the most beautiful, truest, very best kind of glow.

Do you have a dream you always wish to have?

Someone you wish to see?

If so, don't be shy.

As you lie down to sleep, think of that person or pet. Think of a house or a time or a place that you loved.

Ask them to join you.

Say, "Hey, whatta you say, how about one more W-A-L-K? Let's watch the birds. Let's bathe in a sunset. Let's sing a duet, you know the one. Let's run through the long grass, laughing, chasing rabbits we both know we'll never quite catch. I'll meet you in the meadow, the one in our dreams."

Whisper your request into your pillow, close your eyes, then let it go.

Fall asleep and leave it to the Dreamatics. We'll try our best.

The houselights dim.

The velvet curtain parts.

It's magic time. It's showtime.

It's a dream, made just for you.

Acknowledgments

Thank you, thank you, thank you to the dogs in our hearts and the dogs by our sides. Here's to you . . .

Izzy, Cleo, Earl Musselwhite, Ron Swanson, Hugo, Peach, Zoe, Bry, Paris, Reggie, Claus, Champ, Lucky, Kodak, Kitty, Sparky, Bailey, Taffy, Kelly, Toby, Millie, Odie, Briar, Andrew, Rolf, Otis, Tootsie, Tori, Woody, Amber, Ricky, Shamrock, Piper, Rufus, Fozzie, Ivy, Pear, Winnie, Coty, Trixie, Cassidy, Zoe, Dooley, Ahsoka, Buzzy, Charlie, Lennon, Simba, Banjo, Callie, Chloe, Greta, Marty, Jordy, Jasper, Scout, Remy, Wo-Wo, Brandy, BooBoo, Duke, Hoover, Muffin, Whitney, Gracie, Jack, Stella C., Luna, Harley, Boozer, Bruce, Belmont, Louis, Ivan, Delilah, Stella L., Agnes, Maggie the Dog, Malley, Ajax, Bandit H., Bandit C., Midnight, Nikkianni, Mystic, Koda, Rudy, Dakota Dog, Rosco, Gus, Nash, Biscuit, Magpie, Samson, Huck, Shaggy, Huckleberry, Bear, Zachary, Angus, Nellie, Fiona, Rosie, Marco, Birdie, Archie, Isla, Baxter, Brighton, Shirley, Raindrop, Tilda Swinton, Cody, Lassie, Duke, Laddie, Puddin, Shadow, Harlow, Jezabel, Toby, Oscar, Griswold, Mr. Darcy, Bud, Dozer, Koyo, Moki, Claire, Bella, Bean, Rocky, Denver, Shamrock, Fable, and Indy.